Beautiful STRANGER

A charming British playboy.
A girl determined to finally live.
And a secret liaison revealed in all too vivid color.

BOOKS BY CHRISTINA LAUREN

Beautiful Bastard

Beautiful Stranger

Beautiful Bitch

Beautiful Bombshell

Beautiful Player

Beautiful Beginning

Beautiful BEGINNING

CHRISTINA LAUREN

G

GALLERY BOOKS

NEW YORK • LONDON • TORONTO • SYDNEY • NEW DELHI

Gallery Books
A Division of Simon & Schuster, Inc.
1230 Avenue of the Americas
New York, NY 10020

First Gallery Books trade paperback edition November 2013

GALLERY BOOKS and colophon are registered trademarks of Simon & Schuster, Inc.

For information about special discounts for bulk purchases, please contact Simon & Schuster Special Sales at 1-866-506-1949 or business@simonandschuster.com.

The Simon & Schuster Speakers Bureau can bring authors to your live event. For more information or to book an event contact the Simon & Schuster Speakers Bureau at 1-866-248-3049 or visit our website at www.simonspeakers.com.

Manufactured in the United States of America

10 9 8 7 6 5 4 3 2 1

Library of Congress Cataloging-in-Publication Data

Lauren, Christina.
    Beautiful beginning / Christina Lauren. -- First Gallery Books Trade paperback edition.
        pages cm.
(Beautiful Bastard series) I. Title.
PS3612.A9442273B44 2013
813'.6—dc23   2013034995

ISBN 978-1-4767-5510-6 (pbk.)
ISBN 978-1-4767-5174-0 (ebook)

For our fic girls—each and every one of you—and the wild, real-life love stories you've shared. We started writing because we needed to, but we stayed because of you.

C & Lo

Chapter One

"I'm about to cut a bitch," I hissed, pushing my share of the work away from me. Bennett failed to even look up, so I added, "And by that, I mean *paper*-cut a bitch."

At least this got a tiny flicker of a smile. But I could tell, even after doing this for the past hour, he was still in Wedding Preparation Zone, and would keep robotically working until the entire, unending pile of cardstock in front of him was gone. Our normally immaculate dining room table was littered with Tiffany-blue wedding programs. Across from me, Bennett methodically folded each one in half before moving it to the Completed stack.

It was a simple process:

Fold, move.

Fold, move.

Fold, move.

Fold, move.

But I was losing my damn mind. Our flight left at six the following morning for San Diego, and our bags were all packed but for the four hundred wedding programs we had to fold. I groaned as I remembered we *also* had to tie five hundred blue ribbons around five hundred tiny satin bags full of candy.

"You know what would make this night so much better?" I asked.

His hazel eyes flickered to me before returning to the task at hand.

Fold, move.

"A gag?" he suggested.

"Amusing, but no," I said, giving him the finger. "What would make this night better would be getting on a plane and flying to *Vegas*, getting married, and then fucking all night in a giant hotel bed."

He didn't bother to reply to this, not even a whiff of a smile. It was probably fair to say he'd heard this exact sentiment from me approximately seven thousand times in the past few months.

"Fine," I replied to his silence. "But I'm serious. It's not too late to drop all of this and fly to Vegas."

He took a moment to scratch his jaw before reaching for another program to fold. "Of course it isn't, Chlo."

I'd been playing around—*mostly*—up to this point, but with his words genuine irritation swept through me. I slapped my hand on the dining room table, earning a quick blink from him before he resumed his folding. "Don't patronize me, Ryan."

"Yeah. Okay."

I pointed a finger at him. "Like *that*."

My fiancé gave me a dry look, and then winked.

Damn that man and his goddamn sexy wink. My anger dissipated somewhat and in its place came a flare of desire. He was ignoring me, being a patronizing ass. I was being a bitch.

It was the perfect setup for me to have many, many orgasms.

I looked him over and sucked the edge of my lower lip into my mouth. He was wearing a deep blue T-shirt that was so old and worn, the collar was frayed and—even though I couldn't see it—I knew there was a tiny hole right above the hem that was just big enough for me to slide my finger through and touch the warm skin of his stomach. Last weekend he'd been wearing that T-shirt and I'd asked him to keep it on while he fucked me against the bathroom counter, just so I could wrap it up in my fists.

I rocked a little in my chair to relieve the ache between my legs. "Bed or floor. Your choice." I watched him as he remained impassive, and added in a whisper, "Or I could just climb under the table and suck on you first?"

Smirking down at his work, Bennett said, "You can't get out of wedding preparation with sex."

I pulled back to study him. "What kind of man says that? You're broken."

Finally, he gave me a dark, hungry look. "I promise you, I'm *not* broken. I'm getting this done so I can focus on wearing you out later."

"Wear me out *now*," I whined, standing and walking

over to him. I slid my fingers into his hair and tugged. Adrenaline dripped hot and electric into my veins when his eyes fluttered closed and he suppressed a groan. "Where's all this money you have? Why haven't we hired someone to do this?"

Laughing, Bennett wrapped his hand around my wrist and pulled my fingers from his hair. After kissing my knuckles, he very deliberately set my hand back at my side. "You want to hire someone to *fold programs* the night before we leave for San Diego?"

"Yes! Because sex!"

"But isn't it nicer like *this*? Enjoying each other's company and," he said, lifting his wineglass to take a dramatic sip, "conversing like the happily affianced lovers we are?"

I glared at him, shaking my head at his attempted guilt trip. "I offered sex. I offered hot, sweaty, *floor* sex—and then I offered to give you a blow job. You want to fold *paper*. Who is the buzzkill here?"

He picked up a program and studied it, ignoring me. "Frederick Mills," he read aloud, and I began pulling my shirt up and over my head, "together with Elliott and Susan Ryan welcome you to the wedding of their children, Chloe Caroline Mills and Bennett James Ryan."

"Yes, yes, it's so romantic," I whispered. "Come here and touch me."

"Officiant," he continued, "the Honorable James Marsters."

"If only," I sighed, and dropped my shirt on the floor

before working my pants down my hips. "I'm going to pretend it's Spike performing our wedding ceremony instead of that hilarious gentleman with early dementia we met back in November."

"Judge Marsters performed my *parents'* wedding ceremony almost thirty-five years ago," Bennett chastened me gently. "It's sentimental, Chlo. The fact that he forgot to zip up his pants is a mistake anyone could have made."

"Three times?"

"Chloe."

"Fine." I did feel a little guilty for making the joke, but I stood quietly for a minute, letting my memory of the old, frazzled man take shape. He'd met us at the wedding site when we went out to see it last fall, and got lost on each of three trips to the men's room in under an hour, returning with his fly open each time. "But do you think he'll remember our na—"

Bennett cut me off with a stern look before he realized I was only wearing my bra and underwear, and then his expression went a completely different kind of dark.

"I'm just saying," I started, reaching behind me to unfasten my bra, "it would be at least a *little* amusing if he forgot what he was doing halfway through the ceremony."

He managed to turn his attention back to folding the program before my breasts were exposed; he made a crisp seam as he slid his thumb along the edge. "You're being a pain in the ass."

"I know. I also don't care."

He quirked an eyebrow as he looked up at me. "We're almost done."

I bit back my response, which was to point out that folding the programs was the least of our worries; the next week with our two families together had the potential to be a disaster of Griswold-family holiday proportions, and wouldn't sex right now be a lot better than thinking about that? My father and his two boozy divorcée sisters alone could make us crazy, but add in Bennett's side of the family, Max, and Will, and we'd be lucky to get out of there without a felony under our communal belt.

Instead I whispered, "Just really quick? Can't we take a little break?"

He leaned forward, inhaling between my breasts before moving to the side and kissing a path to my left nipple. "Once I start, I don't relish stopping."

"You don't like interruptions, I don't like delayed gratification. Which of us do you think will get her way?"

Bennett ran his tongue over my nipple, and then sucked it deeply into his mouth as his hands circled my waist, slid to my hips, and then worked together to pull my panties off with a satisfying rip.

Amusement lit up his eyes as he looked up at me from where he sucked at my other breast, and his fingers teased at the juncture of my hip and thigh. "I suspect, my impossible wife-to-be, that you're going to get your way and then I'll finish folding these later while you sleep."

Sliding my hands back into his hair, I whispered, "Don't forget about tying the ribbons on the candy bags."

He chuckled a little. "I won't, baby."

And it hit me all over again, like a warm gust of wind: I *loved* him, madly. I loved every inch of him, every emotion that passed through his eyes, and every thought I knew he had right now but wasn't voicing:

One, that I'd been the one to insist we do as much of this ourselves as we could.

Two, that I was the one to assure him it was fine that every distant relative of ours on the planet had somehow squeezed their way into this wedding event.

Three, that I would never, ever back out of the opportunity to wear my wedding dress on the Coronado coastline.

But instead of pointing out the obvious—that he was the one being a good sport here, not me, and that despite all of my bitching I would never be satisfied with a quick Vegas wedding—he stood, turning to walk to our bedroom. "Okay, then. But this is the last night I'm fucking you before we're married."

I was so buzzed by the "fucking" part that it wasn't until he'd disappeared down the hallway to our bedroom that the rest of his words fully sank in.

Bennett was already undressing when I joined him in the bedroom, and I watched as he slipped the buttons free on the fly of his jeans and pushed them and his boxers down his legs. He reached for the hem of his shirt, eyebrows raised in silent question—*want it on or off this time?*—before I nodded and he tugged it up and over his head. He walked over to our bed, lay down on his back, and gazed at me.

"Come here," he said in a quiet growl.

I stepped closer to the bed but remained out of his reach. "When you say 'the last night you're fucking me before we're married,' do you mean that we are only going to have sex during daylight hours this week?"

A tiny smile tugged at the corner of his mouth. "No. I mean that after tonight, I want to abstain until you're my wife."

An unfamiliar panic rose in my chest, and I wasn't sure how seriously to take him. I climbed onto the bed and crawled over, bending to kiss my way down his chest. "I thought I knew what *abstain* meant, but in this context it sounds like you're telling me on a Tuesday that we'll be together all week but *not* having sex until Saturday."

"That's what I'm saying." Strong fingers tangled into my hair and urged my head lower, to where his cock arched, rigid and slick with his own excitement.

I stopped the path of my lips just at his hips, which rose from the mattress in an effort to meet my mouth halfway. "Why on earth would you want to abstain?"

"Christ, Chlo, stop teasing and put my dick in your mouth."

Ignoring him, I sat up and moved to straddle his thighs so he couldn't easily escape if I decided to inflict some sort of bodily harm. "You're *insane* if you think I'm going without sex for the next four days in the middle of this wedding nonsense."

"I'm not insane," he insisted, trying to pull me higher up his thighs so his man parts could get better access to my woman parts. "I want it to be special. And aren't you the one who wanted a quickie before finishing the wedding prep?" His fingers dug into my hips and he lifted me, pulling me down directly over his cock. "So stop struggling."

But I escaped by digging a finger into the single ticklish spot on his body, between two of his ribs, and with a spasm he released me, shoving my hands away.

I bent to kiss him once on his perfect, perfect mouth. "That was before you suggested that my access to this sincerely ridiculous body of yours expires at midnight. Saturday is our *wedding* night. As far as I know, we only get one of those. How could it not be special, even if you're hitting it like a jackhammer all week long?"

"Maybe I want you a little hungry," he whispered, sitting up beneath me. His mouth found my neck, my collarbones, my breasts. "I want you so hungry for it that you can barely think straight." He grew fevered, grasping at my sides, sucking my skin. I was all too aware of the hard press of him against my inner thigh, and wanted nothing more than to feel him inside, hear his sounds as he grew delirious and lost and urgent.

And then a thought occurred to me. "You mean you want me hungry enough to not care if you rip the ungodly expensive lingerie I bought for the wedding night."

He laughed into my breasts. "That's a pretty good theory, but no."

I knew Bennett Ryan well enough to know that I wasn't going to win this battle. Not here, not yet. With him, I never won with words; I only ever won with actions. I kneeled over him, pulling away and smiling at his short, deep grunt of frustration. But then I turned my body so I could straddle his face at the same time I took his cock into my mouth. He reached for me eagerly, hands splayed across my hips and pulling me down, down, down.

My eyes rolled closed at the first sensation of warmth, of the soft slide of his tongue followed by the seal and suction of his lips. I quickly grew lost in the vibration of his moans, his words muffled against me, the tiny tease of teeth before the suction was back and he grew wilder, and desperate. Below me, he rocked up, urging, and I wrapped my fist around his base, gazing at his length, appreciating its shape and smoothness. I loved the feel of him, the impatient jutting of his hips.

With a wicked smile, I exhaled over the tip of his cock, and whispered, "Your mouth feels so good."

He groaned, pushing up meaningfully, but I simply

moved closer, panting across the thick crown, letting him feel the heated pulse of my breath. I slid one hand lower, cupping his balls and pulling gently as my hand stroked just the lower half of his cock. On the tip, I gave him only air.

He could make me come faster with his mouth than with any other part of him, and already I felt close. The physical sensation chased the pleasure from my own mischief and combined into an urgent warmth, my favorite kind of orgasm: Bennett's mouth on my pussy, with the joy I got from teasing him. My release burned like fire down my back, and up my legs, exploding outward until I really did lose all sense of my movements over him. I was most likely fucking his face, my fist wildly pulling his cock without rhythm or purpose.

He slowed as my body calmed, and kissed my clit, my hip, my thigh, before gently pushing me so that I rolled over onto my back. I slid my hand up my stomach, over my breast, and rested it on top of my pounding heart. I hadn't forgotten that I was probably in trouble for offering Bennett's favorite foreplay without reciprocating, but damn, I needed a minute to relish the effects of the Mighty Bennett Ryan Oralgasm.

"That was so fucking *good*," I mumbled, catching my breath. "I think your mouth is its own Greek god. Tongueseus."

He climbed over me, eyes on fire. "I know what you're doing."

I opened my eyes and let the blurry shape of him form before asking, "What am I doing?"

He moved to straddle my ribs, and I smiled, running my hands up his thighs as he reached for himself, and made a long, slow pull down his length. His voice came out like liquid smoke when he said, "You think you'll win this battle."

"What battle?"

He laughed, and reached for the mattress beside my head, bracing himself as he hovered over me. His cock was only an inch from my mouth and he leaned forward and, with his free hand, rubbed the tip over my bottom lip. Without thinking, I slid my tongue out, tasting the small bit of wetness there. I felt my mouth water, my nipples tighten. I wanted him in my mouth, wanted to see him move in, and out.

He moved back a few inches so I had to watch as he stroked himself slowly in front of me.

"I can see your pulse in your neck."

Swallowing, I asked, "So?"

"*So*," he started, wearing a cocky smile, "I can see how much you want this." He leaned forward again, barely touching his cock to my lips before retreating. "You want it in your mouth." His hand began to move faster, and I heard his breath catch. "You want it on your tongue."

He was right. I wanted it so much my skin felt tight and overheated.

"Not as much as you do," I said, voice strained. "You couldn't go a day without sex."

He paused before leaning back and pushing himself farther down my body. For a single, perfect moment, I thought he was going to spread my legs and angry-fuck the daylights out of me, but instead he tilted his head, looked down at me, and then stood.

"What are you doing?" I asked, pushing up onto one elbow so I could watch him pull on his boxers.

"Proving you wrong."

He walked to the door and disappeared.

"*Why are you so fucking stubborn?*" I yelled after him, and all I heard was his amused snort halfway down the hall. "And—if you recall—I gave you head in the shower this morning so technically you already *had* sex today!"

He's coming back, I thought. *Totally one hundred percent coming back. I can wait it out.*

I lay back, stared at the ceiling. My skin was flushed, and between my legs I felt heavy and fevered. My body hadn't caught up with my brain yet, and still wanted to chase after him, beg him to take me for real this time: man parts in woman parts, moving a lot and very fast.

The sound of the fridge opening cut through the silence in the bedroom, and I bolted upright. Was he getting a fucking *snack*?

Before I could think better of it, I was racing down the hall, completely naked. My feet slipped on the hard-

13

wood floors and I wheeled around the corner just as he closed the fridge with an armful of food.

"Are you fucking *kidding* me right now?" I asked, stopping short only inches from where he appeared to be making himself a sandwich. "You're going to have a fucking turkey wrap?"

He turned to look at me, letting his eyes move from my face and down over every one of my naked curves—the bastard couldn't even hide how much he wanted to fuck right now—before returning his attention to my face. "I suppose until my fiancée stops being a teasing bitch or my dick learns to suck itself, I may as well have a bite to eat."

"But . . ." I started lamely, searching for the best way to suggest he eat *me* again without incurring his sexually frustrated wrath. I scowled at his amused half grin. *"Rude."*

"You want sex, you do it on my terms. Tonight's the night, Mills. Actually," he said, giving me a self-satisfied smile, "tonight is the last night I fuck you while you still have that name."

Now *this* I couldn't let slide. "We haven't exactly agreed on anything in the name department, *Ryan.* I'm still gunning for Chloe Myan and Bennett Rills."

"Tell me when you're ready to get it, Chlo." He held my gaze for several silent beats and then leaned down close enough that all I had to do was lean forward an inch to kiss him. I started to, but he pulled just out of reach. "When you say 'please, Bennett, I *need* it' I'm going to fuck you so hard you won't be able to sit down for days without remembering it."

My mouth opened and closed a couple of times without any words escaping. With a knowing smirk, Bennett turned back to his sandwich preparation.

He hadn't bothered to put a shirt on, and his bare torso seemed to go on for miles. His skin was smooth and even, tan from running shirtless in the spring sunshine. The muscles in his arms popped and tensed as he opened the jar of mustard, pulled at the silverware drawer to retrieve a knife, opened the bag of bread. Such simple tasks, but watching him do it felt like the dirtiest and best porn. I loved his forearms, loved the dark hair, the tan skin, the carve of muscles.

God, what an asshole.

I watched his tongue slip out and wet his lips. His hair was a mess and fell heavily over his forehead. When I let my eyes slide down the length of his body, I saw the one reaction he couldn't hide. He was still so hard his cock pressed against the low-slung waistband of his boxers.

Sweet Jesus.

I opened my mouth one more time and, without looking at me, he bent slightly to the side so his ear moved closer to my lips. A shaky exhale escaped and I squeezed my eyes shut.

"Bennett . . . ?"

"What's that you say?" he asked. "I didn't quite hear you."

Swallowing, I whispered, "Please."

"Please what?"

Please, Bennett, go fuck yourself was there, on the tip of my tongue. But who was I kidding? I wanted him to fuck *me*. So, I took a deep breath and admitted, "Please, Bennett, I need it."

The crash came before I fully registered what happened: with a single sweep of his arm, Bennett had cleared the kitchen island and everything he'd taken from the fridge clattered to the floor. Glass shattered and the knife skittered across the tile and crashed into the baseboard. Bennett crushed me against him, bending to cover my mouth, force his tongue inside, and give me the satisfaction of hearing his deep, relieved groan.

It wasn't playful anymore, it wasn't gentle or careful. It was his arms hauling me onto the island, hands pushing me backward to lie flat on the cold marble, and hold me there with one flattened palm pressed heavily to my sternum. It was his other hand spreading my legs wide, his impatient fist pulling at his boxers. And before I could say how much I wanted it, how sorry I was for teasing— because I *was,* and something about seeing him so wild and primal scared me deliciously—he was easily pushing inside, so deep, and then pulling out just as fast, moving his hips in perfect, punishing stabs.

Releasing the weight of his hand from my chest, he grabbed my legs and took a step closer, pulling them over his shoulders and hitting that spot so deep that I felt the force of him reverberate up my spine. He slid his hands down to my hips, and held me in place while he fucked, head thrown back, taking *his* pleasure now. The island was sturdy enough to weather the force of his movements, but I reached over my head, gripping the edge so I could press myself even farther onto him. It wasn't enough; I needed more, and deeper, and wetter, and rougher. He'd told me I couldn't have this for days, and he knew better than anyone that his touch was the one thing—the *only* thing—that could keep me from disintegrating into a hurricane of stress. I needed to get him farther inside me than I ever had before, and I grew obsessed with the idea that I could, somehow.

"God, you're fucking *soaked*," he groaned, opening his eyes to look at me. "How can I keep from taking you? You'll never know how much I need this."

"Then why?" I asked. "Why tell me we can't?"

He bent down, bringing my legs with him so the front of my thighs pressed tightly to my chest. "Because it's the only time in my life I'll be able to stop, to slow down, to relish just being near you." He gulped at the air by my neck and then licked the skin there; his tongue, his teeth, his touch felt like fire. "I want to not be thinking the whole time about where I can take you to be alone for ten minutes, for fifteen, for an hour. I don't want to resent anyone for keeping us apart, while they're there to celebrate," he said, gasping quietly. "I'm obsessed with you, and with *this*. I want to show you I can be measured."

"What if that's not what *I* want?"

Bennett buried his face in my neck and slowed, but I knew his body well enough to guess that he was just on the cusp of losing it, of reaching that point of no return. He ground against me, found that place, and that rhythm that distracted me from my question and made me chase the feeling building between my legs.

I was trapped beneath him and he began to focus on my pleasure, pushing into me and against me, getting me there until I was clutching at his shoulders, digging my nails into him and meeting his thrusts from below. My back was sore and the countertop was stony and cold on my spine but the increasing urgency of his movements made me not care. I could be bruised from it, and it didn't matter. I didn't want anything else but to fall apart with him inside and for him to fall with me.

When my orgasm hit, the sensation that took over my body was a silvery thrill unleashed across my skin, sliding over and inside until I wasn't sure I could handle the feeling of being filled, of being ravaged, and coming so hard I saw black. I screamed, pulling him tight, needing to feel the full weight of him over me.

His movements sped and grew wild and then he arched away. "Fuck!" he shouted, his voice echoing off the vaulted ceiling as he came, freezing over me and hold-ing still. *"Fuck!"*

Despite the chill of the countertop, we were sweaty and breathless. Bennett pushed himself up, and contin-ued to slide in and out, slower now. As if he didn't want to stop even if he had to, he pressed and retreated, eyes moving across my flushed skin.

He'd come already, but he didn't seem to be *done*. In-stead, he looked like a predator who'd had a small taste and now wanted to take stock of what was in front of him before diving back in. I loved this side of him: the Bennett who seemed to barely grasp control, who seemed so unlike his composed, daylight self. His eyes were dark and almost unseeing. Hungry hands touched the friction-warmed place between my legs, up over my hips, up my sides to where they roughly teased my nipples. His hands surrounded my breasts and squeezed, plumping me for his mouth as he bent and sucked forcefully at my skin.

"Don't leave a mark, you menace," I said, and my voice sounded tiny and hoarse. "My dress . . ."

Pulling back, he looked at me and his eyes cleared at this reminder that we lived in a world with other peo-ple, and that we would be required to interact with these other people in the near future for our wedding. A wed-ding where I would wear a strapless gown that would show all of the bite and suck marks he was about to de-liver.

"Sorry," he whispered. "I just . . ."

"I know." I ran my hands into his hair when he trailed off and pulled him over me, wishing we could stay like this forever: me on my back on the kitchen counter, him standing and leaning over me.

He exhaled deeply, pinning me beneath his weight. Suddenly he seemed exhausted. The last few months he'd not only helped with every stage of the wedding planning, but he'd also done everything he could to keep me sane and it *had* to wear on him. I ran my fingers into his hair and closed my eyes, loving this reminder of Bennett as mortal, as a man who could—and *did*—become worn-out or needed a reminder to be gentle. He was the perfect lover, the perfect boss, the perfect friend. How could he manage it? I'm sure some days he just wanted a quiet girl-friend, a woman who didn't argue with every thought he had. A tiny thread of doubt slipped beneath my skin and wove its way into my brain, but then I stopped, feeling my lip pull up in a smirk.

Bennett Ryan was a perfectionist, demanding, stubborn, power-hungry asshole. Any other woman would last about two seconds with him before he chewed her up and spit her out.

And hell, some days I would love a pliant manservant, but no way was I trading in my Beautiful Bastard.

He stood, kissing down between my breasts and, with a reluctant groan, pulling out of me. Bending, he reached for his boxers and slid them back up before looking me over, eyes raking across bare, damp skin.

"I'll finish the programs and tie the goddamn candy ribbons," he said, running his hand over his face. "You've got a kitchen to clean up if you want more of that in our bed later."

"Uh, no," I protested, pushing up on one elbow. The kitchen was a disaster. "I'll do the programs."

"You'll do the kitchen," he said, voice firm. "And hurry, Miss Mills. Mustard stains."

CHAPTER TWO

We'd been in San Diego exactly two hours and I was already regretting not taking Chloe up on her Vegas elopement.

As if equipped with some kind of Bennett mood ring embedded in her brain, the woman in question turned in the seat next to me. I could feel the weight of her attention, her pressing gaze as she watched me and tried to dissect each frown or sigh.

"Why do you look nervous?" she asked finally.

"I'm fine," I answered, aiming for disinterested but failing spectacularly.

"The grip you have on the steering wheel would suggest otherwise."

I frowned more deeply and immediately loosened my hold. We were on our way to dinner, where the majority of our two families would be meeting for the first time. They had flown in from all over the country: Michigan, Florida, New Jersey, and Washington, even some from Canada. A number of them I hadn't seen in twenty years or more. In all, there were over three hundred and fifty people arriving within the next few days. God only knew what we were in for. On a good day I hated small talk. The week before one of the biggest events of my life, I was terrified I would be such an enormous asshole that everyone would leave town before the actual event.

Leaning forward so I would glance over at her, she asked, "Aren't you excited for this week?"

"Yes, of course. I'm just dreading tonight a little, and wondering how I'll handle all of the socializing."

"My guess is 'badly,'" she said, poking my shoulder.

I exhaled a laugh, giving her a playfully stern glance. "Thanks."

"Look, just wait until you meet my aunts," she said, leaning over and kissing where she'd poked me. "It'll be all the distraction you'll need."

Chloe's dad had traveled from North Dakota with his two very loud and eccentric sisters. They were both recently divorced, and Chloe promised me they had the potential to be the biggest disaster of the week. I wasn't so sure we should give out that tiara just yet—Chloe had yet to meet my cousin Bull.

"You'll forget about everything else and all you'll be able to worry about is what they'll do to get themselves arrested and how much it will cost you in bail money. Trust me, it'll be very liberating." She leaned over and began fiddling with the car stereo, stopping on a pulsing, high-pitched pop song. I slid my eyes over to her, concentrating a lifetime of disgust into the brief glance.

Satisfied that I was sufficiently annoyed, she sat back in her seat. "So what else is bothering you? You're not getting cold feet on me now, are you?"

I leveled her with a look that was meant to imply *Are you insane?*

"Okay," she laughed. "Then talk to me. Tell me what else is on your mind."

I reached for her hand, twisting her fingers with mine before resting them both on my thigh. "It's just the looming chaos," I started with a shrug. "This wedding has turned into such a *thing*. Do you know I had fourteen texts from my mother waiting for me when we landed? *Fourteen.* Ranging from *where to get coffee in San Diego,* to *whether Bull could get his back waxed at the hotel*—as if I know! You said it yesterday: it's become its own entity. I can't believe I'm saying this but I wonder if you had it right when you suggested sneaking off to Vegas."

She gave me her trademark gloating smile. "I believe I said 'run.' Run to Vegas. As in *flee*."

"Right."

"You know, we're not that far from the airport," she reminded me, motioning out the window to where we could still see planes landing and taking off. "It's not too late to escape."

"Don't tempt me," I said, because as much as I suspected we were careening headlong into disaster, I didn't actually want to leave. San Diego had always been special to us: it was where I stopped being an idiot and finally let myself love her. It was where *Chloe* finally let me. And Jesus, had it really been over two years? How was that even possible? It felt like only yesterday I was covertly ogling Miss Mills' ass as we checked into the W. Later, she'd called me by my first name, for the very first time.

We'd been back together one other time, of course, to select the location for this weekend. But that had been such a whirlwind trip, and this one carried a far greater weight. We were here for our *wedding.* Despite the way she'd crashed the bachelor party, the fact that we'd bought a Manhattan apartment together, or the ring on Chloe's finger, it was this strange moment of nerves that made it finally sink in. We were getting married. When I left here again, Chloe would be my *wife.*

Holy shit.

I reached up, ran a shaking hand across my clammy forehead.

"You're being awfully quiet over there. Can I take your contemplative silence to mean you're actually *considering* fleeing?" Chloe asked.

I shook my head. "No way," I said, tightening my grip on her hand. "We're here. And there isn't a chance in hell I'd miss seeing you walk down that aisle. I've fought way too fucking hard for you."

"Knock it off, Bennett. You're a lot easier to deal with when you're being a dick."

"And I put up with way too much of your shit," I added, grinning when I felt her fist connect with my shoulder. "But I do feel I should warn you one more time. Some members of my family are a bit . . ."

"Nuts? As in, building a vitamin-manufacturing facility in their garage? As in, paying tens of thousands of dollars for advertising in the AARP magazine?"

I blinked over to her. *"What? Who did that?"*

"Your cousin Bull," she answered, shrugging. "Henry told me some stories on the phone the other day. Apparently it's his new venture. He's going to make a pitch this week for some financial backing from Will and Max."

"Why am I even surprised?"

She waved her hand dismissively. "Families are supposed to be a handful, Bennett. Otherwise you'd never leave them. And mine isn't quite all there, either. You know my aunts are . . . let's just say they're really going to enjoy the Ryan family gene pool. I hope you packed your running shoes."

"Well—" I began, but stopped as she crossed her legs in front of her. "Chloe?"

She picked some nonexistent lint off her nonexistent stockings. "Hmm?"

"What in the fuck are you *wearing*?"

"You like?" she said, lifting her foot and moving it from side to side. Her shoes looked positively dangerous. Spiked heel, deep blue patent leather.

"Were you wearing those when we left the hotel?"

"I was. You were on the phone with your brother."

I wasn't one to catalog everything Chloe wore, but the familiar stirring in my pants told me I'd most definitely seen these shoes before—over my shoulders, if I wasn't mistaken. "Where have I seen those?"

"Oh, I don't know." She was a rotten liar. "At home?"

At home, in our bedroom.

The dirty little box we kept under our bed. The things we did when that box was out.

I remembered the night she wore them, almost two months ago. We hadn't seen each other in weeks and I couldn't get close enough, touch her enough, fuck her hard enough. She'd pulled out those shoes along with something new she wanted to try: a bottle of self-warming wax. I could still remember the heat as she'd dribbled it along my skin; the way goose bumps began at that warm puddle of wax and radiated out, spreading along my body. She teased me for so long I actually promised her I'd kneel and hand-feed her breakfast the next day. I came so hard I almost blacked out that night.

"You're doing this to fuck with me, aren't you?" I asked. "This is about the let's-wait-to-have-sex-until-after-the-wedding thing, isn't it?"

"Absolutely."

We found a parking spot about a block away from Barbarella in La Jolla and I stepped out, walking around to open Chloe's door. I took her hand and watched as she climbed out of the car—tan legs that went on forever, shoes you could easily impale yourself on—and shook my head at her the entire time.

"You're a demon," I said. "I feel like a bride guarding my virginity before the wedding."

"Well, then feel free to give it up, Ryan," she said, pushing up onto her toes to kiss me.

I groaned but somehow managed to pull away, both of us looking in the direction of the restaurant. "Here we go . . . "

———

With the patio area open and visible from the street, we could hear our fathers talking before we'd even made it in the door.

"You need to make sure they sit together," Chloe's dad was saying.

"Nonsense, Frederick, they'll be fine." My father, always the diplomat. "Susan put a lot of thought into the seating arrangement and she knows what she's doing. I'm sure your sisters are wonderful ladies. Let's spread them around a little, give the others a chance to get to know them."

"'Spread them around'? I don't think you understand, Elliott. My sisters are *crazy*. They're man-hungry and newly single. They will hunt down every available male within a six-mile radius if you give them the chance."

I stopped Chloe at the threshold, placing a hand on each of her shoulders and looking into her brown eyes. "You ready for this?" I asked.

She stood up on her toes and pressed her warm lips to mine. "Absolutely not," she said against my mouth.

I took her hand and we stepped inside just in time to see my father laugh. "Don't you think you might be exaggerating a little?"

Frederick sighed. "I wish I were. I—"

"It's about time," Henry said, cutting in front of them to walk toward me. Both fathers looked in our direction as Henry continued, "I was worried you two wouldn't show up and I'd have to drag you naked from your hotel room."

"That's a horrifying image," I said, hugging my brother. "And for the record, I'm having you banned from our floor."

"Bennett," my father said, hugging me next. "Frederick and I were just discussing the seating arrangements."

"And what a disaster it will be if we split up Judith and Mary," Frederick added, directing his words toward Chloe.

Chloe hugged my dad and then moved on to hers. "This isn't going to win me any points with Susan," she told my father, "but I have to agree with my dad here. Keep them together; we don't want them taking over more real estate than necessary. There will be fewer casualties that way."

With that settled, I pulled my dad to the side to give Chloe a moment alone with Frederick.

My mother had rented out the entire beachside restaurant, and I had to admit it was perfect. Tucked away in a quaint little neighborhood, meticulously maintained boxwoods lined the walk and flowering vines and greenery clung to every available surface. Now that the sun was starting to set, the huge outdoor seating area twinkled with strings of tiny lights. The tables were beginning to fill, and I realized I couldn't identify half the people who were smiling in our direction.

"Who the hell are all these people?" I asked.

"Perhaps a little louder, son. Your great-grandmother might not have heard you," he said. "And they're family. Cousins, aunts . . . first nephews twice removed." He furrowed his brow as he took in the line beginning to form at the open bar. "Actually, I'm not sure I even know. Those ones are already drinking, so they must be from your mother's side of the family." He tightened his grip on my shoulder. "Don't tell her I said that."

"Great. Everyone else here?"

"I think so," Dad said. "Your uncles are out on the patio. I haven't seen your cousins yet."

I winced inwardly. My brother, Henry, and I spent the majority of our summers growing up with our two cousins, Brian and Chris. Brian was the oldest of the four Ryan boy cousins and a quiet, serious child, much like I had been. He and I had always been close. But Chris—or Bull as he insisted on being called—made me want to chew off my own limb to escape. My mom used to say that Chris only wanted to be like us, and preferred the nickname so he would be one of the B's: Brian, Bennett, Bull. I always suspected this was bullshit. After all, Henry started with an *H*, and the personalized beer cozy Bull brought to parties, along with his unbuttoned shirt and gold chains nestled in a thicket of wild chest hair, suggested he was totally fine being his own person. Chris just liked the idea of being called Bull because he was an idiot.

"I'm sure Bull is excited to see you," Dad said with a knowing smile.

"I'll keep an eye out," I said. "And I'm sure Lyle has remembered a couple of colorful navy stories he'll pass along to you over dinner. Maybe the results of his last prostate exam?"

Dad nodded, eyes twinkling in restrained amusement as he waved to someone across the room. Dad's eldest brother, Lyle—Bull's father, go figure—seemed to have no filter for the inappropriate. Over the years I'd lost count of the number of stories Lyle had told about his adventures in the navy, disgusting bodily functions, how people in rural towns had "relations" with animals, and the various moles his wife had to have removed from her back. "Maybe I should suggest he offer one as a toast?"

Laughing I said, "I'll give you one whole American dollar to suggest it, Dad."

My mother approached, kissing my cheek before licking her thumb and reaching to smear off what I could only imagine was a bright pink lipstick mark. I ducked out of her grasp and grabbed a napkin off a table instead.

"Why didn't you wear the blue suit?" she asked, snatching the napkin from me to wipe my face clean.

"*Hi*, Mom. You look beautiful."

"Hi, darling. I liked the blue suit much better than this one."

I looked down at the charcoal Prada suit I wore, smoothing a hand over the front of the jacket. "I like this one." *And,* I didn't add, *I packed at two in the morning under a drunken sex haze.*

"Blue would have been more appropriate for tonight." She was practically vibrating with nerves. "This one makes me think you're heading to a funeral."

Dad handed her his cocktail and she downed it with a shaking hand before walking away again.

"Well, that was fun," I said and Dad laughed.

Chloe joined us—clearly a bit exasperated from dealing with her father—and we made a circuit of the room, greeting everyone who had come early in the week and reacquainting ourselves with old family and friends. A little while later, my mom called to let us all know that dinner was starting and we moved back to the dining area.

I located the place cards with our names near the center of the room. Chloe sat on my right, her dad next to her. My dad had apparently taken Frederick's advice because Chloe's aunts—Mary and Judith—were seated together nearby, slapping the table and cackling up a storm. Chris . . . *Bull* made his entrance as we were all taking a seat, shouting my name and lifting his can of beer—and requisite cozy—in my direction. His eyes moved over Chloe slower than should have been humanly possible, after which he gave me a thumbs-up.

I made a mental note to call a friend of mine at the IRS and have him audited.

I was only kidding. Mostly.

Dinner consisted of seared salmon and heirloom toma-toes, potato puree, and basil beurre blanc. It was perfect, and made it almost possible to tune out the conversations around me.

"Are you kidding?" Bull yelled from across the room at an elderly second-aunt on my mother's side. "You must be kidding me. Eagles fans live their life feeling like they never get the credit they deserve. You want attention and praise? Win a *goddamn game*, that's what I'm saying!" Bull took a giant gulp of beer, swallowed, and semi-stifled a loud belch. "And another thing—you're old, I bet you know the answer to this: why the fuck is *Wheel of Fortune* still on? Did you know they have a goddamn website where you can dress up Vanna White? Dress her up like she's some sort of fucking paper doll. Not that I know from experi-ence, mind you." He made a point to meet the eyes of ev-eryone unlucky enough to be seated at his table, whether they were listening or not. "But what the fuck is that all about? And I'll tell you what, she might not be getting any younger, but if I could find someone as hot as that woman to walk around the lot, motioning to the cars like she does on the TV?" Here he made a dramatic flourish with his hand, the other one cocked on his hip as he motioned to the empty space next to him. "I'd make a goddamn for-tune."

"Jesus Christ," Chloe whispered in my ear. "That is a train wreck and a half right there."

I swallowed a large pull of my drink before saying, "You said it."

"You grew up with this guy?'

I nodded, wincing as I downed the rest of my red wine in a single, burning gulp.

"Has he always been like this?"

I nodded again, sucked in a breath, and wiped my mouth with my napkin. I watched as Chloe glanced around the room, first to my cousin Brian, who would be considered by most to be handsome and who had always been fit. Then to my dad and his brothers, Lyle and Allan, both still pretty good-looking for their age. She turned briefly to Henry and then to me, before blinking back to Bull. I could practically hear her evaluating the genetic map in front of her.

"And we're sure there's not a leak in the Ryan family gene pool? Like, is there any way he's the milkman's kid?"

I barked out a laugh that was so loud, almost every head in the restaurant turned in my direction. "I need another drink," I said, standing in a way that momentarily left my chair wobbling on its two back legs.

My phone insistently buzzed in my pocket and I pulled it out to see a flurry of texts from my mother:

Sweetie, your hair is a mess.

They're serving the DeLoach Pinot? I thought we had the Preston carignane set for the table wine.

Tell your father to stop introducing Aunt Joan as the Prospector. I have no idea why she's wearing so much gold nugget jewelry, but he's being rude.

I had just escaped to the bar for a shot of Johnny Black and to scope out all easily accessible exits—I loved my family but Jesus Christ, these people were fucking nuts—when I felt a tap on my shoulder.

"So you're the one who's marrying our Chloe."

"If she doesn't get wise and escape before the ceremony," I said, turning to the women behind me. In an instant, I knew who they were. "You lovely ladies must be Chloe's aunts."

The one to my right nodded, and her entire head of fluffy red hair nodded right along with her. "I'm Judith," she said, and then pointed to her sister. "This is Mary."

Judith had hair that could only be described as some sort of sugary confection: overdyed and overteased into what resembled spirals of strawberry cotton candy erupting from her head. It could have been merely the power of suggestion, but I swear she even smelled like strawberries. Her skin was still relatively smooth considering her age— mid-sixties, if Chloe was correct—and her brown eyes were sharp and clear as she considered me. Mary shared many of the same facial features as her sister, but her hair was a much more subdued, subtle brown, and piled high on her head in some sort of bedazzled and bobby-pinned twist. And while Judith was tall like Chloe, stopping just below my chin, Mary was barely pushing five feet, and was probably as wide through the chest area as she was tall.

I reached out to shake each of their hands. "It's nice to

finally meet you both," I said, smiling politely. "Chloe's told me wonderful things."

They were having none of that and each pulled me in for a squeezing and rather *lingering* hug.

"Liar," Mary said with a cheeky smile. "Our niece is a lot of things, but full of false compliments, she is not."

"She's told me she used to spend summers with you. I believe the phrase she's used most frequently is 'they're a hoot.'" I left out the phrases *cougars* and *bat-shit crazy*.

"Now *that* I'll believe," Judith said with a snort.

"And how are you ladies enjoying San Diego?" I asked leaning back against the bar. I could see Chloe out of the corner of my eye, and just as I expected, Bull had taken it upon himself to fill my seat and keep her company in my absence. A part of me wanted to be her knight in shining armor, and rescue her, but a larger part knew better: if there was one woman who absolutely did not need rescuing, it was Chloe.

"Oh we're having the time of our life," Judith said, sharing a meaningful look with her sister. "Or at least we will be. Did you know this is the first time we've both been single in over thirty-five years? This town doesn't know what's about to hit it. We're going to make up for lost time—or die trying."

I couldn't help but laugh. I was certainly beginning to see that blunt honesty was a Mills family trait.

"So, what's the plan then?" I asked. "You two going to spend some time on the beach and break a few hearts?"

"Something like that," Mary said, winking and doing a little dance to the music overhead.

Judith moved to stand next to me at the bar, leaned in, and lowered her voice. "Tell us about your family," she asked, eager, bright eyes moving around the room. "Just the one brother? Any uncles? Anyone single?"

I shook my head, laughing again. Frederick had nailed it. "Just the one brother and sorry, other than the one cur-rently talking to my fiancée"—they looked over to Bull and deflated a little—"everyone's spoken for."

"My oh my oh my my *my*," I heard Judith say, voice sud-denly soft and low. I followed her gaze to the front door, where Will and Hanna had just arrived. There was a lot of giggling in that corner of the room, where Hanna had practi-cally been tackled by Chloe and Sara, leaving Will to stand by and watch, wearing that stupid grin he never seemed to shake anymore. I missed his ironic scowl. I missed his in-sistence that we were a bunch of pussies. God, he was the biggest fucking pussy now.

He looked up to find me watching and, apparently able to read the giant I TOLD YOU SO in my expression, flipped me off. And suddenly, even though I knew it was wrong and Chloe would kill me when she found out, a plan began to blossom in my mind.

I mean really, how could I not do this?

"Who is *that*?" Judith asked in a breathy rush. I wasn't sure if I'd ever actually *heard* someone leer before, but I fig-ured that was as close as I was ever going to get.

"That's Will," I said. "He works with Max, the Brit with the pregnant fiancée?"

"Is he available?" Judith asked at the very same moment Mary said, "Is he straight?"

I could feel my conscience poking at me, nudging. Some small, shriveled part of my brain was trying to stop me from what I was about to do, insisting this was absolutely not a good idea.

"Oh, he's definitely straight," I said. *Not a lie.* "And he's a lot of fun, ladies. A lot of fun." *Technically not a lie.*

Mary pressed up to my side, asking "Who's the girl with him?"

"That's Hanna. She's . . . an old family friend," I said finally. *Still not a lie.* "You should go over and introduce yourselves."

"So he's not married?" Mary asked, compact already out and mouth shaped in a little O as she reapplied her lipstick. These women were determined.

"Married? Noooooooo. Definitely not married." *What? Not a lie.*

"Hot damn," they both said in unison.

I glanced quickly around the room before wrapping an arm around each of their shoulders, bringing them closer and bending to speak. "I'm going to tell you two a little secret, but it's got to stay between us." I looked at each of them individually and they nodded, eyes wide as they hung on my every word.

"Our Will? He's a bit of a wild boy. He's insatiable, and he's got quite the reputation for his skill, if you're catching my drift. The thing is? He likes *ex-pe-ri-enced* women,"

I said, emphasizing each syllable. "And he likes them in *pairs*."

They both sucked in a breath and looked at each other. I had a feeling a huge telepathic conversation passed between them before they blinked back to me.

"Understand?" I asked, glancing between them.

"Oh, we understand," Mary said.

There was no way I wasn't going to hell.

I watched as Judith and Mary cut a line straight for Will. Hanna, Chloe, and Sara had dispersed, leaving him alone.

Alone and vulnerable.

I realized the only way this would work was if I had buy-in from the most important person in the restaurant. I scanned the room, my eyes stopping on Hanna as she emerged from the back, smoothing her sapphire-blue dress down over her sides.

I practically sprinted over to her.

"How are you?" I blurted out too loudly and far too enthusiastically to someone who had just stepped out of the restroom.

She let out a small gasp and stopped dead in her tracks. "Bennett," she said, pressing her hand to her chest. "You scared the *shit* out of me."

"God, sorry. I just wanted a chance to talk to you before you got swallowed up by the girls again."

"Um, okay . . ." she said, looking around us and clearly confused by my laser-focus attention.

"How was your flight?" I asked.

Her posture relaxed and she smiled, attempting to look over my shoulder to where Will was sitting, probably chin-deep in cougars if my guess was correct. I shifted to block her view.

"It was—" she started.

"Good, good," I said, realizing too late that I hadn't let her answer. "Look, I wanted to mention something to you," I said. *Play it off as casual. Play it off as no big deal. Be cool.*

Her lips curled up in an amused smile. "Okay?"

"You know what a horrible prankster Will can be." She nodded and I continued: "I may have just done something to get back at him and I swear," I said, resting a hand on her shoulder, "I swear, Hanna, you'll think it's hilarious . . . eventually."

"'Eventually'?"

"Absolutely. Eventually."

She considered me through narrowed eyes. "This is just a prank, right? No shaved heads or scars?"

I pulled back to study her. "That was a very specific question. *Scars?*" I shook my head, clearing it. "And no, no, no, no. Just a silly little prank." I gave Hanna my best smile, the one Chloe said made panties drop. But apparently it only made Hanna more suspicious.

Her eyes narrowed further. "What would I need to do?"

"Nothing," I said. "You'll probably see some weird stuff but just . . . go along with it."

"So, basically be oblivious."

"Exactly," I said.

41

"And this will be funny?"

"Hilarious."

She thought about it for a full ten seconds before reaching out to shake my hand. "You're on."

———

Hotel Del Coronado was built in 1888, and stretched across the fine-sand beaches of Coronado Island. With its striking red turrets and blindingly white buildings, visiting here felt a lot like being dropped in the middle of a Victorian postcard. Chloe and I had stayed a few months ago while scouting out possible wedding sites. One glance at the ocean from the balcony of our hotel room and Chloe was sold; this was where we would get married.

As we drove back from dinner that night, my nerves prickled to the surface again, but for an entirely new reason. Chloe was smart—smarter than I was, if I was being honest with myself—and she'd watched me carefully all night, studying. Now, as we neared the hotel, she might have been sitting quietly in the passenger seat at my side, but there was no way she was merely taking in the passing scenery. If I knew her as well as I thought I did, she was planning, silently plotting how to take me down.

Which was why I had a plan myself.

We made the last turn and arrived back at the Del. The crisp white buildings were lit from every angle and practically glowed against the dark sky. I patted the small bottle in my pocket and looked down at my watch, realizing this was either the smartest thing I'd ever done or the stupidest. We'd find out soon enough.

I pulled to a stop at the curb, reached for my bottle of water, and practically vaulted from my seat, desperate for air that didn't smell like Chloe's perfume, and for just a moment of space to gather my thoughts. I washed the Plan down with a giant gulp of water. I had about ten minutes before I should probably be upstairs.

Drawing in a much-needed breath, I handed the keys to the attendant and rounded the car, smiling as I took Chloe's hand.

The hum of voices and gentle tinkling of music greeted us as we stepped into the lobby and crossed to the elevator. I couldn't help but think back on the last time Chloe and I were here together: of fucking her on the huge king-sized bed until she'd screamed my name, of holding her hands behind her back as I bent her over the balcony railing, the crashing waves and rustling palms the only sounds masking the noises she made.

I followed her into the elevator and like some sort of homing device, my eyes dropped straight to her ass. She knew it, too, because there was a much more deliberate swivel to her hips, an intentional shake with each step. I felt myself begin to harden and realized that if this plan went to shit, I was screwed. Literally.

Get your head in the game, Ben, I told myself, reaching

to press the button to our floor. It wouldn't be that hard, I reasoned: keep your distance, eyes above her shoulders at all times, and for God's sake, no arguing about *anything*.

"Everything okay over there, Ryan?" my lady-adversary said, leaning against the wall opposite me. She crossed her arms over her chest and her breasts pressed together. *Danger.* I quickly averted my gaze.

"Absolutely." I had this. I was a genius.

"You look mighty proud about something. Fire someone today? Kick a puppy?"

Oh, I see you, Mills. I see you. I kept my eyes fixed on the mirrored doors opposite me and answered, "Just thinking back on the card Sofia made for us. She must have made it with that cute little art set we bought her for her fourth birthday. But I just realized her handwriting reminded me a lot of yours."

A small, knowing smile pulled at her mouth and she nodded, glancing up at the display as the floors ticked past.

Almost like a weight had been placed on my shoulders, drowsiness began to seep into my limbs and back; my arms felt dense with a heavy wave of fatigue. I smiled wider.

The elevator stopped on our floor and I watched as she stepped out and made her way down the hall. She waited while I opened the door to our room and then headed straight for the bathroom.

"What are you doing?" I asked. What had I expected? For her to strap me down, throw me against a wall, and force me to have sex with her? And why did that sound so damn appealing?

"Just getting ready for bed," she said over her shoulder, and closed the door behind her.

I stood for a moment before moving to open the balcony, feeling the first yawn creeping up. Dinner had gone better than expected. Well, that was a bit of a stretch. Bull made a fifteen-minute meandering "toast" about family, relating several stories about some questionably harassing interactions he had with one of my high school girlfriends before soliloquizing at length about how beautiful Chloe is. My mother sent me seven more text messages I still hadn't read. Judith and Mary ended up sitting on Will's lap, grinning widely at me, and Henry made a circuit of the room after dessert, making a handful of secret bets with wedding guests.

Still, the police hadn't been called and nobody had found themselves in need of emergency assistance, so it was as close to a success as this group would get for our first night out. At least the chaos had taken my mind off Chloe and the shoes she'd previously only worn during sex, and the dress that seemed to show everything but in fact showed nothing—which was infinitely sexier.

I never would have expected to be avoiding sex the week of our wedding. But I'd had plenty of time to think about it while folding what seemed like a million wedding programs, and decided that for the first time in our relationship I wanted to savor *her:* her laugh and her words and the mere reality of her company. I wanted to be able to watch her without thinking about the next time I'd have her naked and up against a wall. It seemed like a good idea at the time, and I'd be lying if I said it wasn't also about wanting to piss her off a little and I knew her well enough to know that with-holding sex would . . . I blinked over to the bathroom door. Where the fuck *was* she? As my lids grew heavier and Chloe took longer doing who-knows-what in the bathroom, I wasn't sure I'd have the physical strength to fight her off if it came to that tonight.

Taking a seat in the living room, I picked up a maga-zine, feeling myself grow more and more tired with every minute. I looked up at the sound of a door opening and nearly fell over. Chloe leaned against the wall, hair loose and falling in wild waves along her shoulders and down the length of her back. Her lips were glossy and pink, and I could imagine that color smeared down my chest and along the skin of my cock. She wore what was easily the sexiest and most complicated lingerie I'd ever seen. The black demi-cups barely covered her breasts; the rest con-sisted of a series of black satin ribbons crossing strategi-cally over her torso and down between her legs. It took me two attempts to finally speak.

"Was someone in there with you?" I slurred.

Her brows came together and she shook her head. "What?"

"Because . . . I have no idea how you got that thing on by yourself." My voice sounded thick and slow. "Hell, I have no idea how I'd even get it off." I held up my hands and they felt heavy and numb. I wouldn't even be able to rip paper tonight.

"That sounds like a challenge," she said with a pleased smile. My eyes moved over every inch of her body and I seemed unable to pull them away. She was fucking *beautiful*. Her legs were long—*so long*—and her feet were still strapped in the same blue shoes she'd been wearing at dinner.

She took a step toward me, and then another. "Do you remember the last time we were here?" she asked.

"I'm trying not to."

She pressed a hand to my chest and easily pushed me farther into the back of the couch before straddling my lap. "You fucked me on the floor . . ." She leaned forward, kissed my jaw. "And the balcony"—she kissed my neck—"and the bed, and the floor and the bed and the floor."

"And don't forget the chair in the corner," I mumbled, hissing in a breath as she scratched her nails over my stomach, reached for my tie, loose but still hanging from my neck.

"What if I said I wanted to re-create some of that?" she whispered into my ear. "What if I asked you to tie me up with this? Spank me? Fuck me in th—"

I yawned. *Wide.*

She jerked back and looked at me, taking in my slumped posture, the way I could barely keep my eyes open. Hers narrowed.

"What did you do?" she asked, suspicious.

I could only smile—a stupid, drowsy, lopsided grin. "Took out a little insurance policy," I slurred. "You're very pretty by the way, and I really do like this . . . thing you're wearing and would like to request that you wear it for me again . . . someday."

"What did you *do*, Ryan?" she repeated, louder, and stood up, hands on her hips as she frowned down at me.

"Just only took a tiny little sleeping pill," I said, yawning as I pulled the small bottle from my pocket, holding it up to show her. "Teensy tiny."

I had a prescription for these for international travel but had yet to use a single one before this. I was actually amazed how fast they worked, and slightly uneasy over the prospect of having no control over my state of arousal. Especially since Chloe looked like she might castrate me.

"You son of a bitch!" she yelled, pushing on my chest. It was sort of a counterproductive move, however, because I merely slumped over, sinking facedown into one of the cushions. She started to yell about . . . something, but I couldn't quite make it out. I took comfort knowing someday she'd know I was really doing this for her.

The last thing I saw before my eyes closed was her storming out of the room, shouting something about payback.

Finally, Bennett: 1; Chloe: 0

Chapter Three

He didn't cave and bang the daylights out of me last night. In fact, he'd gone so far as to drug himself and be taken out of commission. Clearly it was time to up my game.

I'd spent much of dinner last night watching Bennett be adorably mischievous while steering my rascal aunts toward an unsuspecting Will. I'd watched him be jealous and irritated in equal measure when Bull regaled me with stories of the many cars he'd sold and women he'd banged. I'd watched Bennett with adoration as he greeted his family, waited until his mother's food was in front of her before starting in on his own, thanked each waiter personally, and stood when I stood to go to the bathroom.

Bennett Ryan was a swoony fucking bastard, and tonight—stupid chastity rule or not—I was going to ride him like a horse.

I had a suitcase full of lingerie and outfits that were guaranteed to bring him to his knees. Most of the skimpy, lacy things had been reserved for the honeymoon, but I suspected at this point we wouldn't have much need for any form of clothing once we hit the private resort in Fiji.

In a way it was nice to have a new mission. Instead of stressing about our families and the chaos we were diving into headlong, I could focus on the fact that Bennett really just needed to fuck me a few times a day. It was a simple goal, really. I couldn't control the tides or the insanity of our families, but I could definitely control this man's cock.

Will had named this evening the Final Night of Freedom. Even though it was Thursday and the wedding was Saturday, he declared that the rehearsal on Friday all but sealed Bennett's fate as a married man, so he and Max had planned a night out for all of us in the Gaslamp Quarter. We were going to hit a few bars, have a few drinks. As Max put it, "Tonight we're going to get right pissed and pretend Chloe didn't hand each of us a to-do list five miles long."

I'd ordered the guys to get ready in our suite and the women—Sara, Hanna, my childhood friend Julia, soon-to-be sister-in-law Mina, and I—were getting ready in Julia's room. I did this in part to have some girl-time before we all went out together, but also so that Bennett wouldn't see me until we got to the bar. If he saw what I was going to wear out tonight, he would tie me to the bed with one of my slips and change my clothes *for* me.

If I'd harbored any suspicion that he would tie me to the bed and *fuck* me, I'd be happily changing upstairs in the wedding suite alongside him. Alas. I knew Bennett, and I knew how determined he was once he made a decision about something. Tonight needed to be a sneak attack. I had to seduce my fiancé, and in order to do that, I had to play dirty.

Julia and Mina were both working on Hanna's broken zipper, and I sat on Julia's bed and carefully crisscrossed the long, strappy heels up my calf. Last night's shoes had worked pretty well, but obviously not well enough. Tonight I'd put on a tiny black dress, dangly chandelier earrings, and the same shoes I'd worn the night I went out clubbing in San Diego when Bennett and I had been here together for the JT Miller Marketing Conference early in our "relationship".

I tied the satin strap at the back of my calf and thought back to that night, and how Bennett had looked, almost two years ago now, when I'd walked into the hotel lobby of the W in the early hours of the morning to find him sitting on a couch, waiting for me.

His hair had been a disaster, and I knew without having to ask that he'd been pulling at it, nervously running his hands through it. In hindsight it was obvious we were in love even then, but I remembered how surprised I'd been when he admitted he needed another night with me. I wanted it more than anything, but I never expected him to ask for it so openly.

I'd followed him up to my room and in that bed we'd made love for hours, sharing words about real histories and real desires and real feelings. From there, our relationship climbed to a peak—I'd easily stepped up and covered with Bennett's client when Bennett suddenly got sick, and when he recovered, we'd decided to be together, a couple, no more hiding.

"Chlo?" Sara asked, ducking to meet my eyes and pulling me out of my thoughts. "You okay?"

I bent and focused on the other shoe, nodding. "Yeah, just remembering what it was like when the BB and I were first together."

She sat and put an arm around me. "Is it weird to be getting married here?"

Shrugging, I admitted, "A little. It's bittersweet, you know?"

"When did you first know you loved him?"

I closed my eyes and leaned into her, humming as I considered the question. "I think I probably *felt* love for him before I *knew* I loved him. But, do you remember when we were here for the conference and he got food poisoning?"

Beside me, Sara nodded.

"Well, after I did the whole Gugliotti presentation and came back to tell Bennett how it went, I went back down to the conference for a little bit to walk around and let him rest. When I came back up to my room, Bennett was sitting on the couch. He always looks good, of course," I said, laughing when Julia wiggled her eyebrows at me, "but he just looked like a *guy* right then. He was shirtless and his hair was messy in that bed-head, unintentional way. He was zoned out on the television with his hand tucked under the waistband of his boxers. And I had this epiphany that he *was* just a guy, and that he was sort of becoming *my* guy, you know?" Around me, my girlfriends all nodded. "I think those are the moments I love the most, when I look at him and see him as so much more than the Beautiful Bastard. In his BB moments he still feels sort of unattainable and intimidating even to me. Don't get me wrong, I love that side of him. But when we're alone he lets his guard down and I get to see *all* sides of him, and that day was the first time it really happened. I think that's when I knew I loved him."

"I think it was earlier," Mina said, bending to dig into the hotel room minibar. "I saw your face when I busted you in the bathroom at his parents' house. He said being with you was a mistake. Your expression was the reaction of a woman with *emotions*."

I crinkled my nose, considering this. "God, but he was such an asshole then."

"He's *still* an asshole," Mina reminded me. "And I'm pretty sure if he wasn't, you'd find a way to push the buttons to get him back there."

"I like watching you guys," Hanna said. "I've never seen a couple like you before. Seriously, I bet the sex is unreal."

Hanna had been around us so much in the past few months, this blunt-force honesty surprised no one . . . except Mina.

"Don't need to hear it." Mina covered her ears. "Again," she added, glaring at me.

Hanna looked gorgeous tonight, in a silky gray A-line dress that hit just above her knees. Julia had put Hanna's sandy brown hair up into a complicated twist, and her neck was long and smooth, decorated simply with a tiny diamond pendant that rested just at the hollow of her throat. I couldn't wait to see Will try to maintain his trademark poker face when he saw her.

"You have to let me order all the drinks tonight," Sara said, standing and smoothing her shimmering blue dress over her round belly. "I swear to God, I want nothing more than to walk up to the bar tonight and order ten shots, just to see what the bartenders say."

"Pregnancy suits you, Sare," Julia noted, standing and walking across the room to fetch her heels. She sat on the edge of the bed and slipped them on her feet, still staring at Sara. "I like the tummy *and* the attitude."

"I agree," I said. "She's turning into a bit of a hellcat."

Sara laughed and studied her reflection in the mirror for a beat before walking over to have me fasten her necklace. "I just really love my body like this. Is that weird? I like how curvy I am."

"Etienne certainty didn't," Julia said with a snort. "I still can't believe what a fit he threw about having to alter the design of Sara's dress."

I groaned. *The Dress.* Julia had found the most perfect bridesmaids' dresses I'd ever laid eyes on. They were a swirl of beautiful blues—dyed to slowly transition between the Tiffany blue that permeated the décor of the wedding, and a deeper, slate blue. The dresses were made with pleated chiffon and a delicate strap that met over one shoulder, but Sara's, obviously, had to be altered to accommodate her growing stomach. Etienne, the designer, had thrown a tantrum. He'd ranted about fabric draping, symmetry, and lines and even threw in the term *bulbous belly*. It had taken a lot of screaming on his part and a lot of money on mine, and six alterations to finally get her dress right, but it was done. And I couldn't *wait* for my glowing, giddy, *beautiful* maid of honor to wear it.

"I bet Max likes your pregnant body, too," Mina said, giving Sara a knowing smile.

"Oh, he does," I answered for her, untwisting Sara's necklace at the back of her neck. "I feel like I'm watching something indecent even when he's just pouring her a glass of water."

Sara's cheeks turned crimson and I laughed, loving how pregnancy made her completely unable to hide her blush.

"Are we ready to head out?" Julia asked, draining the last of her minibar vodka tonic. "I need to get my drink on."

We all made our way to the door, filing out one at a time. Down in the lobby, Mina had the valet call us a car, and just as I climbed in and closed the door, I saw the men emerge from the lobby of the hotel.

"*Jesus,* Chloe," Julia breathed, looking at Bennett at the front of the group. "Look at that man."

And with my lip pinched between my teeth, I could only nod in agreement. As usual, he'd barely paid any attention to his hair and it was in the usual, completely fuckable disarray. His lips were curled up in amusement at something Will had just said, and when he lifted his chin to nod at the valet, I caught sight of the sharp, edible line of his jaw. He wore jeans and a black T-shirt that wasn't tight but managed to showcase the definition of his body beneath the soft cotton-cashmere blend. I knew this shirt well; I bought it for him and planned to steal it and make it mine in a couple of years after he'd worn it to the perfect state of tattered.

Seducing him tonight would be a *lot* of fun.

My legs were hidden from view, and from his vantage point all Bennett would see was the very top of my tiny black dress.

"You're in so much trouble," Sara murmured next to me, staring down at my heels. "I'm actually hoping I'm there to see his reaction."

"I know!" I said, giddy.

Bennett's eyebrow went up in a silent question and I held my hand out the window, giving him a breezy wave: no, we weren't waiting for them.

"Meet you at Sidebar on Market!" Julia yelled out the window, and Bennett raised his hand, wearing his trademark amused smirk.

———

Sidebar was gorgeous, with rich red and black leather seating, enormous mirrors and sensual nude photos on the walls, and bright red birdcages hanging from the ceiling. The main bar was expansive, made of gleaming marble with a simple filigree pattern decorating the front. The bar was busy but not full when we arrived, and we immediately claimed two large booths toward the back of the room.

The men hadn't been as quick to arrive from Coronado, so we had time to order drinks and return to our seats before they showed up. I looked to the door just as Bennett led the group inside, with Max, Will, Henry, and Bennett's cousins Chris and Brian trailing at the back. But when I stood to greet them, and Bennett's eyes raked over me, from my red lips to my siren red toenails, I knew I was in deep, deep trouble.

I ignored the pressure of his attention as best I could, but with him it was nearly impossible. His focus was a physical presence, a heavy weight on my neck, my breasts, and most of all, the long expanse of my exposed legs. We stood and greeted our friends, and I felt my chest grow tight, my heart race with how fun it was having everyone together. I kissed Brian, Will, and Max and greeted Bull with a brief-but-polite hug.

Only then did I look Bennett over more slowly, and felt a familiar warmth spread from my stomach and down between my legs. Stretching on my tiptoes, I kissed the corner of his mouth. "Hi. You look good enough to lick tonight."

He returned my kiss, stiffly, and then leaned to press his mouth to my ear. "What in the fuck are you wearing?"

Glancing down, I smoothed my hands over my sleeveless, beaded black minidress. "It's new. Do you like it?"

Before I could look up to catch his reply, Bennett grabbed me by my upper arm, pulled me down a dark hall, and shoved me against a wall. Even in the dim light I could see the rage and lust on his face. My favorite fucking Bennett. Arousal rose in me; every inch of my skin ached to feel his fingertips.

"What the fuck do you think you're doing?" he growled.

"Could you be more specific? I'm having a drink, I'm out with some friends, I'm—"

Both of his hands came up, roughly pinning me by my shoulders to the wall. I let out a tight moan, and his eyes narrowed further. "The shoes, Chloe. Explain the fucking *shoes.*"

"They're special to me," I said, slowly blinking down to his mouth. I licked my lips as I stared at his, and he leaned in closer, instinctively. "Something old, something new. I wore these once when we were here together. Do you remember?"

Just as I suspected, his face grew impossibly more angry. "Of *course* I remember. And the 'something old, something new' is for the actual wedding day, not the entire week before when I'm trying to keep my hands off you."

"I'm practicing," I said, breathless. "In fact, there are a lot of things I'd like to practice before the wedding, Bennett. Like deep-throating."

"Are you really trying to break me?"

I shook my head with wide, innocent eyes but said, "Yes. I really am."

His grip on my shoulders lessened and he slumped forward, resting his forehead against mine. "Chlo . . . You know how much I want you every second."

"I want you, too. So, I thought maybe later we could go back to the hotel and I could keep the shoes on? You could have me on my back, legs in the air . . ." I turned, kissed the shell of his ear. "Plus, I have this amazing corset on under here and—"

Bennett pushed away and turned, storming down the hall.

I took the opportunity to sneak into the women's room to check my makeup and high-five myself in the mirror. But my martini wasn't getting any colder, and I had some seducing to do, so I didn't linger long.

Bennett seemed to have calmed himself by the time I returned to the table, and was sitting in the booth with Max and Will while the other men ordered drinks at the bar and the women danced a few yards away from where we sat. Bennett's arm was slung over the back and I slid in beside him, running my palm from his knee to his upper thigh. "Hi," I said again. "Having fun?"

He gave me a look that would have melted the face off a lesser opponent, and I grinned, leaning to kiss his neck and whispering, "I can't wait for you to come in my mouth later."

He coughed, practically dropping his vodka gimlet onto the tabletop, and earning a few curious looks from Will and Max across the table.

"You okay over there, Bennett?" Will asked, knowing grin in place. Had Bennett told the men about his newly donned chastity belt? I hoped he had; no one would be happier to help me in my plan to derail Bennett's determination than Will and Max.

"Just went down the wrong pipe," Bennett explained.

"He's usually much better when he's aiming it down mine," I said in a stage whisper, and both Will and Max burst into laughter across the table. Will leaned forward to give me a high-five.

"Has he told you about his new virginity?" I asked.

"He mentioned he's enjoying the sport of keeping you waiting," Max said. "But for the record, Chloe, I'd like to say that those heels are fucking smashing."

"I agree!" I said, grinning over at my fiancé.

The booth was large enough for several people, and after they'd ordered their drinks, Brian and Bull joined the four of us. For several quiet moments we sipped our cocktails, and Max and I shared an amused grin when we heard Sara's cackle across the room.

"That's your girl over there," I said.

He raised his glass to me, cheeks flushed, and murmured, "Indeed it is," before taking a sip.

I looked over at Sara and laughed. "Actually, that's your girl over there with a big belly . . . carrying a tray of shots."

He looked up and groaned, standing to walk over. His words drifted out of earshot after we heard him say, "Sare, love, that's too heavy . . ."

"He is *whipped*," Will murmured.

"Don't even start on that, Sumner," Bennett said with a shake of his head. "You can barely keep your tongue in your mouth around Hanna."

Will shrugged and leaned back in the booth, not even hiding the way he looked over at his girlfriend and studied every inch of her exposed legs.

I let my eyes move around the men at the table and wondered if they were being relatively quiet because they wanted me to leave so they could discuss guy things, like penises and basketballs and toilets. But I was so comfortable, and the weight of Bennett's arm around my shoulder was too perfect to want to move. The only way I would move is if it was to climb into his lap and wiggle a little.

I started to execute this brilliant idea, but he stopped me with a tight grip on my shoulder. "Don't you *dare*."

"Are you hard?" I asked quietly, just loud enough for him to hear.

He shot me a look. "No."

I licked my lips and felt my pulse take off when his eyes dropped to my mouth and he leaned a little closer. "How about now?"

"You're impossible, woman." He moved away, reaching for his drink.

A large tattoo of a woman's face on Bull's arm caught my eye and I leaned close to Bennett again, but he leaned away.

"No, come here," I said, pulling at his T-shirt. "I have a question. I swear I'm not going to lick your ear." Reluctantly he leaned close enough for me to quickly lick his ear before asking, "Who is that on Bull's arm?"

He studied it for a second before turning to whisper, "I think that's his girlfriend—or ex-girlfriend?—Maisie. They've been on-again, off-again since they were teenagers."

I absorbed this information: Bull might currently be

"on" with this Maisie woman and was hitting on every vagina under forty in the wedding party. "Are you kidding me?"

"I wish."

I studied it as casually as I could; the last thing I wanted to do was raise Bull's attention and let him think I was checking him out. But the tattoo was enormous, practically the size of my entire hand, and incredibly detailed. It had been hidden at the dinner the night before under his dress shirt, but now, in casual clothing, the entire thing was revealed, in full color. Basically, it was Maisie's face, neck, and chest stopping just where the hint of her breasts began to swell.

Turning back to Bennett, I whispered, "Jesus. She must be bringing it. I know how to suck a dick but no one has ever tattooed my face on their skin."

Bennett went still, hand frozen where he had just reached for his glass.

"I don't expect you to tattoo *my face* on your arm, Mr. Ryan, settle down."

He exhaled heavily, bringing the glass to his lips and saying, "That's good," before he took a sip.

"But I would like to suck your dick so hard you promise to do it anyway," I said and laughed as he planted his hand on my back and shoved me out of the booth, telling me to go play with the girls for a bit.

We danced, and drank; Hanna and Mina were an unstoppable combination of inappropriate, and had all of us laughing until our sides hurt on the dance floor. It was a perfect night: out with all of my favorite people in the entire world, surrounded by my girlfriends while the love of my life hate-loved me with fiery intensity from across the room.

And, because they were fully on my side in this ridiculous abstinence business, Max and Will came and joined us and surrounded me, dancing and teasing, lifting me up and carrying me to Bennett for an upside-down, drunken kiss.

"I love you anyway," I told him as he scowled down at me. "And I'm going to break you tonight."

He shook his head, giving in to the smile he was trying to fight. "I love you anyway, too. And you can try your hardest, but it won't work. You're not getting my dick again until we're married."

We brushed our teeth side by side and studied each other in the mirror. I was wearing a thick cotton robe over my weapon of mass seduction, but Bennett wore only his boxers, so I took some time to appreciate his naked torso. I loved his man nipples, the dusting of hair on his chest, and the definition of his shoulders, chest, and stomach. I lovingly counted the six-pack and then stared at the trail of hair leading from his belly button to beneath his boxer briefs. I wanted to lick that line and then taste the smooth skin of his cock.

"Did you take a sleeping pill again?"

He shook his head, mouth wide as he brushed his back molars.

"I like your body," I said around a mouthful of toothbrush.

He flashed me a foamy toothpaste smile. "Likewise."

"Can I give you head?"

He bent to spit and rinse his mouth before saying simply, "No."

"Want to give me a quickie from behind?"

He wiped his face on a towel and then placed a peck on the top of my head. "No."

"Handie?" I asked to his retreating form as he left the bathroom.

"No."

I washed my face and walked out into the bedroom to join him. He was already under the covers, reading some political nonfiction book.

"I'm going to try to not be insulted that there's a military man on the cover of that book and you just turned down a blow job."

"Let me know how that works out for you," he said, giving me a little wink.

Shrugging, I stripped out of my robe and stood near him, wearing a tiny mint-green thong with a skirt overlay in silk chiffon with delicate floral embroidery and matching sheer bra. Thin silken garters held up the softest nude stockings I'd ever worn.

He glanced up and did a quick double take, exhaling, "Christ," under his breath.

"Just some comfy jammies," I said, hopping over him and climbing under the covers. "I just love sleeping next to you when I'm wearing silk garters and these flimsy, *expensive* panties."

He adjusted the pillows behind his back and returned to his book, but I counted to one hundred before he even turned his attention from one page to the next, so I could tell there was no way he was actually reading anything.

Sliding the covers down to expose my upper thighs, I curled into his side, humming. "You should feel these stockings. They're so *delicate*. I bet you could just look at them and they'd rip."

Bennett coughed, and then smiled patiently down at me. "I'm sure they would. I bought them for you, after all."

"But I'm just not sure I should sleep in them." I frowned thoughtfully. "Can you help me take them off?"

He hesitated for a beat, staring at his book before turning and placing it carefully on the bedside table. And then he peeled the blankets all the way off my legs and studied me in the muted light of the table lamp.

"You're so fucking beautiful," he murmured, bending to kiss my neck, my collarbone, and the top swell of my breast.

Victory exploded with adrenaline in my veins and I closed my eyes, arching my spine so he could unclasp my bra, lifting my ass so he could carefully remove the tiny skirt around my panties. But I opened my eyes, studying him as he gently peeled the stockings down my legs, planting only a single kiss on the inside of each knee.

Something was off.

When I lay only in my panties, Bennett looked up at me and smiled wickedly before grasping them and sliding them down my legs, dropping them *undamaged* on the floor beside the bed.

"Better?" he asked, stifling a laugh.

I glared at him, trying to burn a hole in his forehead with my eyes. "You're a prick."

His eyes danced. "I know."

"Do you know how much I want to feel you on top of me? Did you not *see* that lingerie? It was ridiculous! You could have ripped it with your *teeth*!"

"It was stunning." Bennett bent and kissed my mouth so sweetly, so fully, that my chest squeezed almost painfully in pleasure. "I know how much you want it. I want it, too." He nodded to his shorts, where he was so hard I could see the tip of his cock pressing up from beneath the waistband. "I'm asking you to trust me."

He reached to turn off the light, and then turned so that he was on his side facing me. "Tell me you love me."

I ran my hands up his bare chest and into his hair. "I love you."

"Now go to sleep. Tomorrow is a big day. The rest of the guests arrive, we rehearse our wedding, and I am one day closer to being your husband. After that, I will never deny you again."

He kissed me slowly, all firm, warm lips, no tongue, no sounds, just his mouth on mine, sweetly sucking and soothing me until I felt serene, and doted on, and even drowsy enough to imagine I could fall asleep next to this man and not need to be worn-out from orgasms.

I woke up to an otherwise-empty bed. It wasn't an uncommon occurrence, and I started to fall back asleep before remembering that Bennett wouldn't be up working; we were in San Diego for our wedding. My heart exploded in panic and a cold, sick feeling of déjà vu crept into my stomach. What if Bennett was *sick*?

I bolted upright and looked at the light under the bathroom adjoining our darkened bedroom. Climbing out of bed, I moved into the main room of our suite and to the small bathroom adjoining the living area. The light under there was on, and I tiptoed forward, not sure whether I should call out to him or just go back to bed and hope that he was okay.

I blinked, taking a step backward and remembering the only other time I'd seen Bennett sick—the food poisoning incident I'd discussed with Sara earlier.

"Why didn't you wake me up?" I'd asked him.

"Because the last thing I needed was you in there, watching me throw up."

"*I could have done something. You don't have to be such a man.*"

"*Don't be such a woman. What could you have done? Food poisoning is pretty lonely business.*"

Resolved to leave him alone, I started to turn back to the bedroom . . .

Until I heard a quiet groan.

My heart twisted in sympathy and my pulse picked up speed. I moved to the door, putting my hand against the wood. Just as I was about to call out to him, to ask if he needed a Popsicle or some ginger ale, he moaned and sounds of pleasure escaped in his deep voice: "Oh, fuck. *Fuuuuuuuuuuck.*"

I pulled my hand back from the door and slapped it over my mouth, stifling a gasp. Was he . . . ? Did he escape to the nonbedroom bathroom so he could. . . ?

On the other side of the door the faucet turned on, and I stared at the wood as if I could develop X-ray vision if I only concentrated hard enough. How often did he do this? Did he masturbate all the time in the middle of the night? The faucet creaked slightly as he shut off the water and I turned, bolting back into the bedroom.

I hurled myself on the mattress and yanked the covers up to my chin so Bennett wouldn't know I'd moved from where he left me, *sleeping*. Sleeping while he tugged one out in the other room!

I rolled into my pillow, stifling a giggle. In the other part of the suite, the bathroom door opened, and a slice of light cut across the carpet before everything quickly went black when he flipped off the switch.

I listened intently, trying to slow my breathing as he padded across the carpet and back into the bedroom. Bennett carefully lifted the covers and slid in beside me, curling up along my side and kissing my temple.

"Love you," he whispered, running his water-cooled hands over my too-hot skin.

I still hadn't decided if I was going to pretend to be asleep, or bust him for this and give him endless shit, so I sleepily rolled into him, sliding my hand up and over his chest to rest on his heart. His pulse was hammering, racing, positively *pounding*.

Like he'd just had a sneaky, covert orgasm.

I cuddled into him, stretching close to his ear. "You didn't even moan my name. I'm insulted."

Beside me he froze, his hand covering mine on top of his heart. "I thought you were sleeping."

I snorted. "Obviously." I nibbled at his jaw. "Did you have a nice self-inflicted bathroom orgasm?"

Finally, he admitted, "Yes."

"Why did you bother going in there? I have a hand and several orifices at the ready."

With a laugh, he simply said, *"Chloe."*

"Do you do that a lot?" I wondered if he could hear the slight edge of anxiety in my voice.

"I've never done it when I'm with you. I just . . ." He brought my hand to his mouth and kissed my palm.

"You're naked. It's hard to . . ." Laughing, he seemed to reconsider what he was going to say. "It's just been *hard* for a few hours. I couldn't sleep."

I loved his voice in the middle of the night, all deep and gravelly. I loved it even more after he'd had a middle-of-the-night orgasm . . . even if he'd had it from sneaking into the bathroom and stroking himself. His voice was always deeper after he'd come, his words delivered more slowly. He was impossibly *sexier*. "What were you thinking about?"

He paused, his thumb smoothing up and down the back of my hand. "Your legs spread over my face and your mouth on my cock. Like the other night, except without your teasing."

"Who came first?"

With a groan, he said, "I don't know. I wasn't . . ."

I smacked his chest lightly. "Oh please. I know how specific your fantasies are."

Rolling to me in the dark, he said, "You came first. Of course you came first. Okay? Can we go back to sleep?"

I ignored this. "Did you come in my mouth or on my—"

"In your mouth. Sleep, Chloe."

"I love you," I said, leaning to kiss him.

For a moment, he let me take his lip into my mouth and suck on it, nibble it. But then he pulled away and wrapped his arms around my waist, shifting my head closer to his chest. "I love you, too."

"I don't want to get up and go to the bathroom," I said, smiling into the darkness.

I heard his mouth open but it was several seconds before he made a sound. "What do you mean?"

I rolled to my back and spread my legs so one of them was bent and resting on top of his thigh.

"*Chloe . . .*" he groaned.

I found that I was already wet, just from the idea of what he'd done, and what he'd been thinking. I was wet from the memory of his voice in the bathroom when he came: it was the sound of relief mixed with regret, and the fact that I could tell it was more out of necessity than fun made it so much hotter. I slid my fingers over my skin, rocked up into my hand.

Beside me, Bennett held very still until I let out my first quiet moan, and then he shivered and melted against me, rolling so he half covered my body, and ducked to kiss a path from my throat to my breast.

"Tell me what you're thinking," he whispered into my skin. "Tell me every *fucking* thought."

"It's your hand," I said, feeling my pulse quicken with my own strokes, "and you're teasing me."

His voice was so deep it was barely more than a vibration when he asked, "How so?"

Swallowing, I told him, "I want you to touch my clit and you're just dragging your fingers in tiny circles all around it."

He laughed, sucking a nipple into his mouth before

releasing it with a quiet, slick kiss. "Slide just one finger inside. Keep teasing. I want to hear you beg for it."

"I want more." My finger was so much smaller than his, and one of his was never enough. One of *mine* was a torment with that voice in my ear and that breath on my skin. "I want faster, and bigger."

"Such a demanding body you have," he said, sucking on my jaw. "I bet you're slippery and hot. I bet I know exactly how you taste right now."

My fingers circled, still teasing, knowing it's what he would do. What he *wanted* me to do. I pressed my head back into the pillow, whispering, "Faster. Please, more of *something*."

"Both hands," he relented quietly. "Two fingers inside and work the outside. Let me hear it."

I slid my other hand down my body and inched closer to him, feeling the unyielding shape of his renewed erection against my hip. With both hands, I touched myself, relishing the clean sweat and soap smell of him beside me, the rough scratch of his stubble on my neck and chest as he kissed me hungrily, whispering, "*Goddamn* it, Chloe. Let me hear you."

My breath caught as he slid his palm over my breast, squeezing it roughly before ducking to pull the peak deep into his mouth. I loved the sound he made when he suckled me. It was desperate, and rumbling; a sound so rich I could feel it behind my eyes, and in the center of my bones.

"Oh, God," I groaned. "Close . . ."

He released my nipple from his mouth and reached to whip the covers off my body, exposing my skin to the cool air of the hotel room and the blazing heat of his eyes.

"It's my hand you're fucking," he growled. "Show me what you like." I lifted my hips from the mattress, wanting to please him, wanting him to relent and climb over me, claim me as his.

But instead, Bennett slid one of my legs higher up my body so he could reach down and land a sharp smack on my backside. "I'd do better; my hand would fuck you harder than this. I'd make you *scream*."

It was a sufficient stand-in, and with his lips pressed to my ear telling me he was going to fuck me so long and so rough on Saturday that the next day I'd *wish* it'd been my own hand instead, I managed to come, hot and pulsing against my fingers.

But it wasn't even close to what he made me feel.

We fell back against the pillows in breathless, unsatisfied silence.

It wasn't enough to orgasm, and to feel his breath on my breasts and his filthy words on my skin. I wanted to feel his pleasure when he came *in* me, or on me, or simply with me. I wanted to witness every time he felt that moment of release. He was mine; his pleasure was mine, and his body was mine. Why was he making me wait for it?

But as he ran a big, possessive hand from my hipbone

to my shoulder, stopping at every curve along the way, I understood what he was doing.

He was giving me something other than the wedding to think about.

He was being a withholding ass so I would torment him.

He was making me torment him, and pretending to hate it.

He was ensuring that this week would feel like *us*, and we could be outwardly focused on everyone else while staying focused only on each other behind every blink, in every dark room, and in each one of our private thoughts.

Bennett was ensuring that we would see each other at either end of the aisle and know we made the best choice of our lives.

"You're pretty brilliant, do you know that?" I asked, curling into him and running a hand up over his shoulder and into his hair.

He pressed his lips to my neck and sucked. "You can thank me later, Einstein."

He turned his head to kiss me and I groaned into his touch. His lips were so firm, so commanding and I gave in to him as he parted them and pressed his tongue inside, sweeping, searching.

I shook when his hands returned to my skin, warm and rough, feeling every curve and dip, every small hollow. I felt the hard press of his cock against my stomach and tried to roll him on top of me.

"I want you inside," I said. I heard my own voice and it was hoarse and needy. I ran my hands up his neck, cupping his face and trying to pull him closer.

But he inhaled, turned and pulled my fingers into his mouth.

"Fuck," he groaned, taking each of them between his lips and rolling them over his tongue, tasting my sex. He pushed my hand away, sweeping a frustrated palm over his face and rasping, *"Goddamnit."*

"Ben—"

Before I could hold on and keep him there, he'd rolled out of bed and walked back to the bathroom, slamming the door behind him.

CHAPTER FOUR

I could barely open my eyes the next morning.

Bright yellow sun filtered through the open balcony door, warming my skin where it cut across the bed. I could taste the salt in the air; hear the sound of the tide as it washed along the beach. I could feel the heat of Chloe's body where it pressed against my side. Naked.

She mumbled something in her sleep, slipped a smooth leg up and over mine, and shifted closer. The sheets smelled faintly of her perfume and even more of *her.*

With a groan, I extricated myself from her grip and very carefully rolled her to her side. Swinging my feet to the floor, I stood, looking down at my very hard, very selfish dick. *Really?* I thought. *Again?* I'd gone to the bathroom on two separate occasions last night—both before and after Chloe's little one-woman show—and still. Always the traitor.

Chloe thought I was brilliant for having us wait until Saturday, when in reality it was starting to feel like the worst idea I'd ever had. I felt anxious and on edge—aware of a persistent hum beneath my skin and a need for exertion—

to fuck until I was too tired to stand or sit, too exhausted to do anything but fall into bed and pass out.

Under normal circumstances I'd have cut off my right hand before considering leaving a warm bed and naked Chloe. But these weren't normal circumstances, and frankly, my right hand had proven invaluable the last few days.

I'd almost caved last night, and at this point, it would be like surrendering to the enemy. I needed to get out of here.

I found my phone in the living room and typed a message to Max. `I need to run. You in?`

His response came less than a minute later. `Definitely. I'll grab Will and meet you at the main pool in 10?`

`See you then` I typed back, and tossed my phone to the couch.

I'd have time to jerk off, clean up, and escape the room before Chloe was even awake.

Max had most definitely gotten laid. I watched him as he neared the pool, hair a mess and limbs loose and relaxed. It would be easy to hate this guy if I wasn't so damn happy for him.

Okay, no. I still hate him a little.

"You look disgustingly pleased with yourself," I said, dropping into a deck chair beneath a bright blue umbrella.

"And sadly, you don't," he said back with a smirk. "Your virginity giving you trouble?"

I sighed, rolled my neck, and felt the tension that seemed present in every single muscle. "Is it tomorrow yet?"

Max shook his head, laughing. "Almost."

"Where's Will?"

"With Hanna still, I think. He said to wait, that he'd be down in a few." Max took a seat across from me, bent down to tighten the laces of his running shoes.

"This is good. There's something I wanted to talk to you about."

He squinted up at me. "What's up?"

"Do you remember when Will hired that creepy clown to deliver a singing telegram on my birthday?" I asked, an involuntary shudder moving up my spine. This kind of thing had become the norm in the Will, Bennett & Max Show. After having accidentally hired a transvestite hooker for Will while we were all in Vegas, he'd retaliated by having a couple of goons pretend to bust us for card counting. It had only escalated from there. Chloe insisted it was only a matter of time before one of us ended up in the hospital or jail. My money was on jail.

Max groaned. "Fuck. I thought I'd finally erased that mental image. Thanks for bringing it back."

I glanced back toward the hotel to make sure I didn't see Will coming down yet. "I have some retribution in the works."

"Okay . . ."

"Did you happen to meet Chloe's aunts last night?"

"The ones that looked like a couple of hyenas circling a lame gazelle? Yes, lovely ladies."

"I may be partly responsible for that," I said, waiting for his reaction. He seemed completely unfazed.

"'Partly,' Ben?"

"Okay, completely."

He shook his head, but was clearly amused. "You don't think they'll get their hopes up, do you?"

"I got the sense that they were just looking to have some fun. I sort of told them he liked experienced women and that he liked them in pairs. All of which is true, I might add."

He raised a brow.

"*Technically* true," I corrected. "I'm going to hell, aren't I?"

"Did you give Hanna the heads-up?"

"I'm not a total dick, Max." When he lifted his brows as if to say *Oh really?* I ignored him, continuing, "I may have suggested she play along. She agreed."

"That's it? She's easier than I expected," he said, already shaking his head in disbelief. What girlfriend would ever agree to such an evil albeit brilliant plan? Clearly, Hanna was a genius.

"It took a little reassurance that he'd escape unharmed, but yes, she did. I really like her, by the way."

"Same," he said with a quick nod.

"So what do you think? Should I call it off? I'll be honest, I'm feeling a little dirty over this one. They're Chloe's *aunts*."

We heard footsteps move across the deck and both looked up, seeing Will jogging toward us.

Max leaned in quickly and whispered, "Tell him and I'll kill you."

———————

There were surfers scattered down the shore and a few runners passed us as we started away from the hotel.

"So what had you up so early?" Max asked from my right, keeping a steady pace with me. Will, *the competitive runner,* was about twenty feet in front of us, shouting insults and patronizingly encouraging remarks over his shoulder every few minutes.

"Just . . . everything," I admitted. "I don't think I've ever been so exhausted and so keyed up at the same time in my life. You probably don't want to hear this, but I'm not sure whether I want to sleep for ten hours or fuck."

Max gave me a sympathetic pat on the shoulder. "I know the feeling," he said.

"Like hell you do," I said back, looking over to him.

He fought a laugh. "Sorry, mate. I don't mean to mock your pain, and this will most definitely fall into overshare territory . . . but I've never seen Sara like this before. She's always been . . . How should I say this . . . ?" He scratched his jaw, thinking. "She's always been eager. But pregnant Sara? Jesus, mate. I can barely keep up."

I'd really have liked to shove Max into the pounding surf, but I had to admit it was a little endearing to see him so flustered and fumbling through his words. "That might be the most inarticulate thing I've ever heard you say."

"Fucking right."

"Really trying not to hate you," I groaned.

"So, aside from the obvious," Max said, meaningfully. "How are things?"

"The usual. My mother is texting me every half hour with whatever happens to be her worry of the moment. Chloe's dad wouldn't have the foggiest idea where he's supposed to be at any given time without Julia assigned to Frederick Watch. Bull is waiting for Chloe to decide she wants one last fling. I'll probably be checked into rehab by the end of the day."

"And Chloe?" he asked.

"Chloe is Chloe," I said. "She's sexy and infuriating and constantly keeps me guessing. I thought I might strangle her last night but we talked. I think we're finally on the same page."

"Sounds great then," he said. But it was too short, too flat, and I didn't miss the way he kept his eyes trained on Will.

"What?" I asked, watching his expression.

"Nothing."

"If you have something to say, Stella, say it."

Will must have realized we weren't behind him anymore because he'd doubled back. "What's up?" he asked, using the hem of his shirt to wipe the sweat from his brow and looking back and forth between us, clearly confused.

"We're talking about Plan Chastity," Max explained.

"Oh, good," Will said, turning to face me. "If I may, this sexbargo thing may be the dumbest thing I've ever heard."

"I—" I began.

"Agreed," Max interrupted. "I get that it's all a fucking game with you lot most of the time, but who flies to California to get married, rents a bloody suite on the beach, and then doesn't bang the hell out of his hot fiancée?"

"Stupid." Will nodded.

Max gave me a withering look. "Imbecilic."

"Embarrassing to all men, if I'm being quite hon—"

"*I don't know, okay!*" I yelled, my voicing booming down the beach. "I know it makes no sense! At the time, it made sense. 'Make it special,' I thought. 'Make the tension build,' I thought. I wanted her to remember how fun it was to be pissed at me all day every day. I wanted her to remember that there really is only one man who can handle her and it's me, *goddamnit*! Now, it seems like the worst idea in the history of bad ideas. But I'm committed. Do you see this tiny corner I've painted myself into? Do you?"

I gestured around me frantically until both of my friends were forced to give me slightly terrified nods.

"I threw down this gauntlet, I have to follow through. This is *Chloe* we are talking about. She already has her fist curled tightly around one of my testicles, at least let me keep the other one! If I fuck her before Saturday night she's going to think she owns both balls and can wear them as fucking charms on a bracelet. She'll expect me to *thank* her after she sucks my dick! She'll think she's *letting* me spank her! She'll wear shoes to work that no one has any business wearing even in the bedroom!" I took a huge, gulping breath, lowering my voice, "And then. *Then* I will spend the rest of *forever* trying to convince her that she's an ungrateful, pain in the ass, harpy shrew who really just needs to be tied to the bed and fucked until she's thanking me for existing!"

I wiped my chin free of any spittle that may have escaped during my tirade and squeezed my eyes shut, chest heaving.

"You *really* need to get laid," Will whispered in awe.

Max rested his enormous hand on my shoulder. "He's right, mate. This is more serious than I thought."

"Oh, shut the fuck up," I hissed, shoving his hand away and starting to walk down the beach. "It may be my mistake but you're all just as fucked. If Chloe wins this week you're all toast. Every man in the world is toast and will suffer like no one has suffered before. I don't like it—didn't plan it—but those are the stakes we're all now facing."

Max shook his head, falling into step beside me. "It's not just you who needs to get laid, Ben. Chloe hasn't been herself this week, either. Maybe your strategy here is off."

I slowed to a stop again. "What are you talking about? You saw her last night; she was being a royal pain in the ass. How is that 'not herself'?"

"All this marriage business has definitely made you soft if you think *that* was Chloe being a pain in the arse," Max said. "You two are the most volatile people I've ever met. Some days it's like watching two cartoon characters having a go at each other. And the Chloe Mills I've heard stories about would have ripped off your tackle and made you eat it to get what she wanted. She would have tied you to a chair and tortured you until you were begging her to fuck you. What'd she do last night? Wear a short dress? Shake her tits in your direction? That's the same woman that had straight-laced Bennett breaking all the rules and fucking her all over RMG? I don't buy it."

"I—" I started, blinking dumbly.

"Will, tell him your nerdy theory," Max said. "It's really quite brilliant."

Will took a step closer, leaning in conspiratorially. "Have you ever heard of the calm before the storm? That moment right before a tornado or large weather occurrence when everything goes completely still?"

"I think so," I said, absolutely not liking the sound of that and how it could relate to Chloe, but curious despite myself. "Yeah."

Will got this really intense expression, like everything he was about to tell you was the most fascinating thing he'd ever heard. He sort of bent at the knees, using his hands to gesture wildly, dramatically illustrating any point he might have. "So vapor and heat rise, drawn up toward the center of a storm. The updrafts remove some of the saturated air, forcing it up and over the highest clouds. You following me so far?" he asked. I nodded, feeling a thread of anxiety form in my chest.

"He's getting to the fascinating part," Max assured me.

"So you have all this air rising, but it compresses as it

falls, leaving it warmer and dryer. *Calm*"—he said, pausing for effect—"resulting in a stable air mass, dampening cloud formation and leaving the air totally still. The calm before the storm."

Max was already nodding; clapping Will on the back like he'd just explained the most clever analogy ever told.

I frowned. "What are you saying?"

Max reached out, put a solid grip on my shoulder. "What we're saying, mate, is that *you* think you're keeping your bird in check. But we're all waiting for your little bomb to explode."

———

I watched Chloe like a hawk the rest of the day, and as terrified as I was to admit it, Max and Will had a point.

She didn't give me an ounce of fight when I got back to the room and showered alone. When I kissed her bare shoulder, she smiled at me warmly, but without the slightly terrifying look in her eyes like I would either be fucked to within an inch of my life or eaten for breakfast. She was wrapped in a towel, skin still damp from her shower as she blow-dried her hair. She didn't comment on the fact that she was naked, she didn't ask to "help" me get dressed. She didn't ask me to fuck her once.

She was accommodating and loving, and I was completely confused.

When the waiter messed up her order at breakfast, she didn't react. When her aunts insisted on following her around

with a camera, going so far as to film her from the opposite side of the bathroom stall, she stayed calm. When my
mother suggested Chloe wear her hair down instead of up for
the ceremony, Chloe had only responded with a pained smile.

By this point I could practically *smell* the storm in the air,
and we hadn't even started the rehearsal yet.

"What do you mean 'small' accident?" I said, focusing on
the wedding coordinator before quickly glancing to Chloe.
She was about thirty feet down the beach, pacing. A few
swear words had floated back to us at first but now she was
sort of strangely silent, arms folded over her chest as she
walked along the sand.

I frowned, but quickly shot my attention back to our wedding coordinator, Kristin, as she launched into an explana-
tion.

"It's going to be fine, Bennett," she was saying, words
delivered in a way I'm sure I was supposed to find comfort-
ing, but only resulted in pissing me off. When things went
wrong you screamed at someone. You became the loudest
and squeakiest wheel; you let everyone know that anything
less than perfect was unacceptable. You slammed doors
and fired people. You didn't stand there in your little blue
Chanel suit and pearls and tell the cyborg bride and clue-
less groom that it *would be fine.*

"There's been a tiny little problem with the wedding
clothes."

Small accident. Tiny little problem. These adjectives didn't really fit the feeling of dread that had begun clawing its way up my throat. "The garments were dropped off earlier today, but when the bags were opened we realized there'd been some sort of miscommunication and nothing had been pressed. It's a *minor* thing, Bennett. I wouldn't even bother you with it if Chloe hadn't been there and seen it for herself."

So Chloe had already seen bags of wrinkled wedding clothes and hadn't gone nuclear. I sighed, blinking across the beach to where a few rows of temporary seating had already been set up. Chloe's aunts were sitting on either side of Will, who had his hands folded in his lap and looked . . . tense. In fact, he looked a lot like he was deciding if he could bolt and escape this event entirely. Hanna was chatting with Mina but would look over occasionally to glance at him, and her small smile would invariably turn into the biggest shit-eating grin I'd ever seen. She was going to make an excellent ally in the years ahead.

Max and Sara were off . . . somewhere. I actually rolled my eyes when I realized they hadn't made it down from their room yet. God, I hated him. My family stood waiting for the rehearsal to begin, talking among themselves.

"So what happens now?" I asked.

Kristin smiled. "Everything's already been taken back to the cleaners and it will be done in the morning. They've promised to drop everything off tomorrow before one."

"The wedding is tomorrow at *four*," I said, running a hand through my hair. "Don't you think that's cutting it a little close?"

"It shouldn't be—"

"Not good enough. I'll pick them up myself."

"But—"

Having overheard, my brother stepped up and placed a hand on Kristin's shoulder. "Just nod," Henry said. "It's easier that way, trust me."

———

The rest of the wedding party arrived and I made my way over to Chloe. The pacing had stopped and she was sitting on the beach now, her delicate pink dress pulled up the length of her legs, toes buried in the sand.

"You ready to do the rehearsal?" I asked, testing the waters. I reached out and helped pull her to her feet, taking her hand as we walked toward the others. "You seem a little quiet."

She shook her head. "I'm fine," she said simply, and moved to stand where Kristin had indicated.

Okay then. I looked up at the sky, actually expecting clouds to have formed overhead.

The thing that had always driven me crazy about Chloe was that I couldn't ignore her, whether she was in a room, or out of it. It had been that way since the day we met. I wanted her every second of every day, and it pissed me off.

I'd lash out at her for distracting me and she'd dish it right back. This only resulted in my wanting her more. Always.

Even now, standing on the other side of the aisle as we listened to the Honorable James Marsters, our officiant, explain where we would be and when, I couldn't keep my eyes off her.

"Bennett?" I heard someone say, and looked up, surprised to find everyone watching me, waiting. The distinctive sound of Max's laughter floated up from somewhere over my shoulder and I mentally flipped him off. "Are you ready to run through it?" Kristin said, slowly, as if it wasn't the first time she'd asked.

I frowned, annoyed to have zoned out. I was pretty sure it was important for me to know what the hell was going on. "Of course."

"Okay then. Guys?" Kristin said. "Can we get the wedding party to line up?"

A murmur of voices surrounded us and we turned to watch as everyone got into their places near the end of the aisle.

As best man, Henry lined up first, offering his arm to Sara.

"All right, everyone," Kristin announced, "let me explain what will happen. Best man and maid of honor will line up on this section of Windsor lawn. The chairs will begin here," she said, moving down the aisle and motioning to a spot near the edge of the grass, "and move this way up toward the beach. Approximately three hundred and fifty of them—just beyond the two orchid arrangements—which will be placed right here." Kristin reached for Henry and Sara and moved them into their spots. "Okay, first bridesmaid and groomsman?"

Julia stepped forward, but so did both Max and Will.

Max clucked his tongue at Will, reaching out to take Julia's arm. "This lovely one's mine, mate."

"But I thought—" Will asked, searching the area. "Where's my bridesmaid?"

"Right here, pretty boy." I looked behind Will to see our fourth bridesmaid, Sara's assistant, George, step up to the line, and reach for Will's arm.

"You have got to be kidding me," Will said, then jumped and let out what could only be considered a manly squeak as Chloe's aunts passed by, one of them laying a sharp pinch on his ass.

"Looks like you might have a bit of a fight on your hands there," Max said to George. "Those two ladies look like they could take you if things went badly."

"Oh hell no," George said in the direction the aunts had gone. "Those two cougars better watch their Raquel Welch wiglets because until that hot piece of ass and the ice queen are married tomorrow night, Sumner here is *mine*."

"And mine," Mina said, taking Will's other arm. "This lucky man gets both of us."

George leaned over to smile at Mina. "Are you willing to be inappropriate at all times?"

Mina winked. "Every second of every day."

Chloe turned to Kristin. "Will there be an open bar? Like, at the end of the aisle? For me? Can I request that?"

"What is even happening here?" Will said, looking to each of us and then back to wherever the cougars had wandered off to. "Am I drunk? Hanna, they just pinched my ass and this one"—he motioned to George—"wants to claim me for his own. A little help?"

Hanna took a sip off her frilly girl drink, complete with big pink umbrella and some sort of neon glow stick. "I don't know, you seem to be doing pretty well on your own there," she said, then took another long pull of her straw. Hanna really wasn't much of a drinker; I was willing to bet anyone at that resort that she'd be asleep in the sand within the hour.

"Jesus Christ, is everyone on something because I want some of whatever it is," Will grumbled, reaching for George's arm and looping it through his. "And don't try to lead," he told George, before offering his other arm to Mina.

"Now that that's settled," Kristin said with a sigh. "Let's get everyone lined up." The wedding party fell into place and stood quietly, paying attention. For once. "Okay, good. Chloe, you're back here. Father of the bride?"

Frederick took his spot next to Chloe and we moved through the ceremony. Thank God all I had to do was walk my mother to her seat because really, this all seemed very complicated and Chloe's breasts looked amazing in that dress.

When my bride-to-be finally reached me at the altar, I took her hands and we both turned toward the officiant, the increasingly senile older gent with thinning gray hair, and dull blue eyes he had to narrow in order to focus on the text.

Chloe was unusually quiet, nodding in all the appropriate places but not offering anything more. A part of me was beginning to worry that this amounted to more than just a case of pre-wedding nerves. I'd just made the decision to take her aside as soon as we'd finished when the Honorable James Marsters said, "And then I will pronounce you man and wife, and then Bennett . . ."

I watched Chloe's head snap up, her brows drawn together as if she had to have misheard.

"What did you just say?" she asked, waiting intently, and for a moment I thought, *Yes, there's the fire, there's the woman Max was talking about this morning.*

And then I realized what the judge had actually said that got her riled up. *Oh no.*

"Which part, young lady?" he asked, finger moving back over the worn words in his book, attempting to track down a phrase he could have skipped or mispronounced, something to have caused such a quick response.

"Did you say man and *wife*?" she clarified. "Man. And wife. As in, he remains a man but I will now only be referred to as something that belongs to him—no longer able to have my own identity and existing solely as someone's *wife*?"

I heard Max's voice rise above the din of confused murmurs. "Does anyone smell rain?"

James reached forward and patted Chloe's arm above where I held her hands, wearing a fatherly smile. "I understand, sweetheart . . ." he said, turning his eyes to me for help. "Isn't this the version of the ceremony you requested, Bennett?"

Her head whipped to me, eyes blazing. *"What?"*

"Chloe," I said, and tightened my grip on her hands. "I understand what you're saying and we'll make the adjustment. They asked me if I had any ceremony preferences and I only—"

She took a step back, shaking her head as if she couldn't believe what she was hearing. *"You?!"* she shouted in the world's most enormous overreaction, and I was actually a little impressed by how much anger and contempt she was able to form into a single word. "You gave him that? Those are the vows *you* chose?"

"I didn't choose those lines specifically," I said, horrified, albeit admittedly a little turned on by the furious rise and fall of her chest. "But that section was in the—"

"I don't need you to explain anything to me. He's reading from some ancient text that promotes the bullshit idea of patriarchal ownership. A version *you* picked out. I've been to church, *Bennett.* 'Wives, submit yourselves to your own husbands?' Fuck. That. I didn't put myself through college, *and* grad school, *and* an internship all while putting up with your condescending ass just so I could lose my identity and be known only as the little wife. And another thing," she said, taking a much-needed breath and turning toward Kristin, who, could only stand there, frozen, lips parted in concern as if she were worried moving could trigger more Chloe rage. "What the fuck kind of mom-and-pop cleaners drops off thousands of dollars' worth of dresses and tuxedos looking like they just came out of some frat boy's duffel bag?"

Excitement, lust, and the thrill of anger blurred the edges of my vision. "What the fuck do you mean by *my* condescending ass? Maybe if you'd put as much effort into your personality as you did into behaving like a raging bitch all the time, I would have been a little more pleasant to be around!"

"Ha! And by pleasant, do you mean bringing you your coffee and stupid little chocolate Danishes and pretending not to notice the way you were staring at my tits?"

"Maybe I wouldn't have stared at your tits if they weren't in my face all the time."

"Maybe they wouldn't have been in your face all the time if you didn't call me into your little hellhole of an office for every little thing. 'Miss Mills, I can't read the handwriting on this expense report. Miss Mills, I specifically asked that these documents be collated by ascending date, not descending. Miss Mills, I've dropped my pen, perhaps you could bend over and retrieve it from the floor near my chair because *I'm a giant fucking pervert!*'"

"I never said that last one!" I shouted.

She got right in my face, breasts pressed to my chest and eyes full of fire as she met mine. "But you *thought* it."

Fuck yes I did. "I also thought about firing you about seven hundred and fifteen times. Let's hope I made the right choice not acting on that instinct, too."

"You are such an egotistical asshole," she growled.

"And you're still a man-eating shrew!" I shouted back. And God, this was so familiar and felt so fucking good, it was exactly what we needed. I wanted to throw her down, pin her to the sand, and tear through her clothes so I could bite and mark the skin underneath.

I pushed a hand into her hair and she knocked it away, gripping the fabric of my shirt instead to pull me down, kissing me too hard and for too long and with way more tongue than was appropriate considering where we were. A fact I'd only become aware of as the sound of catcalls and horrified apologies began to float around us.

"Oh, my," I heard someone say.

"I think . . . I think they've had a lot of stress in the past few weeks," my mother murmured.

"Jesus this is awkward," said someone else.

"Are they just going to have sex right here or . . . ?" That one was definitely George.

"Who called today?" Henry asked. "Will? Was it you?"

By now, Chloe had wrestled me down to the ground and was starting to climb onto my lap.

"Okay!" My father's voice cut through and I straightened onto one knee, trying to disentangle my hands from Chloe's hair and hers from my belt. "I think we're good here. Kristin? The cars should be out front; it's time for the rehearsal dinner. Let's go, everyone!"

Chapter Five

I felt like my skin was going to ignite. Bennett sat beside me in the car, scrolling through emails on his phone, as calm as he'd ever been in his life. After the rehearsal exploded into chaos and dry humping at the altar, I'd gone upstairs to change, splash some water on my face, and take a few minutes to collect my sanity. But once I was back beside him, I wanted to find something else to yell at him about. I wanted to get into another huge, knock-down, drag-out fight. Unfortunately for us, fighting meant sex and we'd both agreed to the stupid fucking abstinence rule.

Instead, we sat in heavy silence, the memory of the disastrous rehearsal sitting between us like a thick fog.

He cleared his throat and without looking at me, asked, "Did you bring your pills?"

I looked over at him and smacked his hand holding the phone. He slid it back in his pocket, chastised.

"What did you just ask me?"

"Your birth control pills," he clarified. "Did. You. Bring. Them."

I turned in my seat to face him, fire and ice sliding into my arteries and pumping into every part of my body. "Are you fucking kidding me right now?"

"Do I *look* like I'm kidding?"

"I've been taking the pill for ten years without your help, traveling almost half of every week for the past year and a half, and managing to pack them for every god-damn trip without the Bennett Ryan Checklist, and you think you need to verify on how responsible I'm being *now*?"

He blinked away, pulling his phone back out of his pocket. "A simple 'yes' or 'no' would have sufficed."

"How does a 'fuck off' sound?"

Turning his head to me, he said very quietly, "It sounds like you might be playing with fire, Miss Mills."

Heat slid down my torso and up my thighs, meeting at the juncture between my legs as I realized he was intentionally provoking me. No matter how calm he looked, he was just as worked up as I'd been. I shifted in my seat, hissing, "Controlling ass."

"Temperamental bitch."

I leaned in, punctuating each word with a jab of my index fingertip to his chest. "You. Imperious. Overbearing. Tyrannical. *Prick*."

My back hit the floor of the limo hard enough for my breath to escape in a gust, and Bennett's weight was on me fully, his cock pressing into the neglected space between my legs. Shoving my skirt up my hips, he rocked up against me *hard*, his mouth covering mine and forcing my lips apart so he could run his tongue inside and across my teeth. I felt more than heard his groan, the sound vibrating along my tongue and down my throat; my mouth, my hands, my pussy felt the emptiness acutely. I wanted him *everywhere*.

I arched into him, pulling his hair so hard he grunted in pain and with one hand grabbed my wrist, pinning my arm above my head, while reaching between us with the other.

It took two vicious tugs for him to tear my panties off—after all, why wear the skimpy, flimsy ones when I didn't expect him to touch me in southern regions anyway?—and then he was pulling down his fly, freeing his cock, and positioning himself against me.

"Please," I begged, struggling a little for him to release my hand just so I could put both of my hands on his ass and drive the sex from below.

"Please fuck you?" he asked, sucking at my jaw, my neck. "Please make you come?"

"*Yes.*"

His lips moved over my neck, sucking, tasting. "You don't deserve it right now. I just want to . . ." He looked down at me, nostrils flaring. "I want to—"

"And the couple of the evening has arrived!" I heard a muffled voice say out of nowhere.

We didn't even know we'd been stopped at the curb until the door to the limo flew open and Max stood, smiling down at us before his face fell in horror and he slammed the door shut again. Outside on the curb, I heard him proclaim, "Looks like the happy couple just need a moment to finish a conversation!"

Bennett scrambled off me, shoving himself back into his pants, tucking in his shirt and glaring at me. I sat up, pushing my skirt back down and grabbing the shredded tatters of my underwear.

With a pissed-off growl, I threw them at him. "Seriously Bennett? Can't you keep the fetish in check for one fucking night?"

He shook his head, retrieving them from where they'd landed on the seat before tucking them into the inside pocket of his jacket.

I took a minute to check my hair and makeup in my compact mirror while Bennett bent over, elbows on his knees, and tugged at his hair. "Fuck!" he shouted.

"It's your stupid fucking rule."

"It's a *good* rule."

"I thought so, too," I grumbled. "Now I'm not so sure. You've reduced us both to cavemen."

Almost in unison, we took several deep, measured breaths. I leaned to the door, looking back at Bennett with my fingers poised on the handle. "Ready?" I asked.

He let go of his hair and turned to look at me. He

studied my hair, my face. He let his eyes drop to my breasts, my legs, before moving back to meet my eyes.

"Almost." He slid closer, framed my face in his hands before covering my mouth with his. He pulled my lower lip into his mouth, sucking. Never closing his eyes, he looked straight at me, gaze turning from hard and cold to warm, adoring. Releasing my lip, he repeated, "Almost," and then kissed down my chin, my neck, and back up to give me one more, lingering kiss on the mouth.

He was apologizing for being an ass. My apology was letting him do it.

⁂

The Bali Hai restaurant was miles away from the Hotel Del on Coronado, but it was one of Bennett's favorite places in San Diego. Located on the northernmost tip of Shelter Island, the restaurant boasted an amazing view of the entire harbor as well as much of Coronado. The building, which was reminiscent of the Pacific Rim–Polynesian style tiki décor, was two levels, with a famous restaurant upstairs and the large, private event room on the ocean level.

I stepped out of the limo to the now-empty curb (apparently Max had decided it was better that the guests greet us inside instead) and burst into a giddy smile. Although I'd seen photos and had heard all about the restaurant's well-executed menu and world-famous mai tais, I hadn't seen the site yet; Bennett had wanted to organize this dinner for me, much as I'd organized the honeymoon. We'd rented out the entire first floor, and already the party spilled out onto the deck outside. A bar was set up overlooking the water, and another bartender was busy mixing drinks inside. Waiters carrying appetizers walked among the crowd, and every member of our wedding party and family was here for this dinner before the big day. As we stepped deeper into the room, all of our guests turned to cheer.

It was sweet . . . these people were all family and our closest friends, but at my side, Bennett smiled stiffly, thanking everyone. I couldn't exactly blame him for feeling the heavy awkwardness. Who knew how many of these people had just caught a glimpse of Bennett over me, pinning my arm to the floor of the limo, about to ram his cock into me?

At least all of the guests tonight were family or wedding party. They were contractually obligated to pretend like they'd never seen a thing.

As the shouts of welcome died down, I heard the distinctive voice of Aunt Judith rise above the sudden silence as she practically yelled, "That man could fuck me back into my twenties."

Murmurs and uncomfortable laughter broke out around her but, bless her heart, she didn't look even a little mortified to have been caught verbally molesting the groom loud enough for everyone to hear. She simply shrugged and said, "What? He does. Don't pretend like

you don't know what I'm talking about. Our Chloe better have some tricks up her sleeve is all I'm saying."

"Well, you don't see my face tattooed on his arm," I
whispered, smiling sweetly up at Bennett.

With a scowl, he pulled me deeper into the room, making a beeline for the bar. "The mai tais are very strong,"
he cautioned me before leaning forward and ordering one
for himself. "I mean, there isn't anything but alcohol in
them."

"You say this like it's a bad thing." I pressed into him,
wrapping my arms around one of his. Smiling at the bartender, I said, "I'll have the same."

"There sure is a lot of driving this week," Bennett's
uncle Lyle grumbled as he walked up behind us. "Why
can't we just stay put is what I'm asking."

I felt my eyebrows rise in question as I looked up at
Bennett. Not only were we paying for his entire family
to stay in the Del; we'd also hired cars to drive everyone
wherever they needed to go. He squeezed my side in a
patient reminder: *our family is crazy.*

Clearing his throat, Bennett said, "Just a lot of wonderful landmarks to hit, Lyle. Wouldn't want you to miss
out."

Bull swept up to us, his famous beer cozy currently
occupied with a can of Bud Light, and held up double
finger-triggers. "I know what *I'd* like to hit this week."
He winked, made a clicking noise as he pulled the trig-
gers at me. "THAT LADY RIGHT THERE."

"Appropriate," Bennett said dryly in Bull's wake. "Always classy, Bull."

Bull waved over his head and headed straight toward the empty dance floor. The DJ was only just starting out the night with music on the upbeat but quieter side before food and then the real party started, but it didn't seem to matter. Bull moon-walked out to the center of the floor and then started soft-shoeing in circles, beckoning to every woman who dared to make eye contact. "I'm a single stallion this week, ladies. Who's the first to ride?"

Most everyone turned back to their drinks, or whomever they were talking to, or simply looked up at the ceiling.

I took my mai tai and sipped it, before coughing harshly. "Wow, you're not kidding." Bennett rubbed my back as I wheezed, "That is *strong*."

"Oh, please, Chlo," George said as he approached, bumping his hip into mine. "You're man enough to take it."

"More man than you are," I agreed, looking him over. He'd changed from his suit into dressy jeans and a fitted white button-down shirt with intricate black diamonds on it. He looked *fantastic*. I felt my smile wilt a little when I realized there wouldn't be anyone fun here for him to flirt with, except Will, who was taking a much-needed respite in the corner of the room with Hanna. Will looked a little exhausted already from the Adventures of Judith and Mary—he'd finally given in and enjoyed their brand of absurdity, letting them feed him strawberries over breakfast while Hanna laughed—and probably wouldn't even be up for some good George Games anyway. "Looks like Bennett's cousin is out there looking for a dance partner. Are you ready to ride the Bull?"

George's dark eyebrows inched up as he looked over at the man in question, still dancing alone, still working on his own brand of seduction. "Is that my only option for shenanigans this weekend? Having fun with the Jersey Shore contingent?"

"Sadly, I think so," I said. "Unless you want to try to turn Will some more. I just fear you have some cougar competition there, and from what I hear, Hanna is trying to break his penis this weekend."

George took my drink and enjoyed several large gulps before wincing and handing it back, now only half full. "Holy crap that's strong."

"You think *that's* strong," Lyle said, pointing his drink at George, "you should try some of the drinks we had back in the navy."

A tiny grin pulled at the corner of George's mouth. "I bet I would have loved everything about the navy."

"Every single sailor," Bennett said under his breath, sipping his drink. He ran his free hand down my back, coming to rest on the curve of my ass.

Lyle continued on as if no one else had spoken, "Those drinks . . . you'd try them and afterward think gasoline tasted like water. And the hooch would make us randy, oh boy." Beside me, Bennett shifted on his feet, groaning quietly. Lyle nodded, pointing at me. "I'd have to walk around until I found a willing lady, sometimes had to pay for it, but I didn't mind." Lyle looked across the room, raising his drink in greeting to Elliott and Susan. "The drink was that kind of wicked, what can you do?"

I pressed my hand to my lips, struggling to hold back my laugh. "Oh, I don't know, Lyle," Bennett said quietly. "Maybe you could not point at my fiancée when you're referencing hiring prostitutes?"

"That's probably what I would do," George agreed.

Oblivious, Lyle turned back to us. "They'd put a cinnamon stick in it over the holidays. Mark the occasion. Still tasted like fire."

"Cinnamon fire," I added, helpfully.

"In the drink or in the prostitutes?" George asked, brows pulled together.

Lyle didn't even crack a smile. "The drink."

"Really could have gone either way," I said to George.

"I don't know what women taste like with or without cinnamon sticks in them, is what I'm saying," George stage-whispered to me. "Maybe it's a thing."

"One kid from my crew," Lyle started, rolling back into his memories again. "Now what was his name?" He took another drink, closed his eyes, and then opened them in a flash. "Bill. Oh, that Bill, I tell you what. He was something else. One night he drank the hooch and came back wearing women's underwear. Boy, did he get chased around the barracks that night."

We all stood in silence, contemplating this for a few beats before George said, "Like I said. The navy sounds like my kind of place."

We all turned at the sound of a loud shout. Across the room, Will was covering his ass with both hands, giving my aunt Mary his sexy-fire look of *oh-woman-you're-in-trouble* before taking several predatory steps toward her. Mary was covering her mouth in a pathetically inadequate look of contrition.

George looked over at me. "Should I be jealous that someone else is harassing my boy toy?"

"Very," Bennett mused dryly. "I'm surprised Chloe's aunts haven't put a saddle on him yet."

"Well, then maybe I need to go find him and tell him once he goes gay, there's no other way. I think he'll be particularly interested to hear about what these magical hands can do." He wiggled his fingers suggestively in my face.

Lyle turned, drink in hand, and gave George a quizzical look.

"To a keyboard. Do to a keyboard," George added, winking at me before walking across the room to the dance floor.

⌐───────⌐

On the patio, Bennett and I looked out at the water, and chatted with some distant cousins he hadn't seen in years, and whom I'd never met. They were nice enough, and the conversation entered the familiar territory of most conversations this week:

How's the weather been in _____?

Now what is it you do again?

When was the last time you saw Bennett?

The entire time, his hand was around my waist, gripping me as if I was being punished.

His rough touch pissed me off, and thrilled me. Sliding my hand over his, I carefully dug my fingernails into the back of his hand. He squeezed my side harder and I dug in deeper. With a small yelp, he let go of my waist, glaring down at me.

"*Damnit*, Chloe."

I smiled up at him, sugar sweet and giddy from winning the tiny battle, and felt Max's giant hand cover my shoulder as he leaned between Bennett and me to speak to the wide-eyed cousins. "Don't mind them. This is how they show love."

The DJ announced that dinner was ready, and we all filed in to find our seats. Bennett and I were seated at the front of the room, sandwiched between our parents and flanked, farther down, by the entire wedding party.

I could still feel the echo of Bennett's hand on my side, and it *ached*. But more than that, it felt cold and hollow. He was the only man I wanted so desperately that I pissed him off just to relish the satisfaction of watching him crack and give in to me.

Elliott and my father stood and walked to the front

of the room. Elliott smiled at the DJ as he took the microphone. "Bennett is my youngest, and his entire life he has been driven, restrained, and poised. When Chloe came into my life, Bennett was still living in France. At the time, I would have no idea what she would do to my son's composure."

The room filled with quiet laughter and murmurs of agreement.

"I *hoped*, mind you," he said, looking at me. "It was hard to know you, darling, and not want you to belong to us in some way. But, especially with these two, you can't force anything. They are forces of nature. I'm so happy for you both, and I'm happy for Susan and myself, Henry and Mina. It feels a bit like the world has settled down the right path when you two are together."

My father took the mic when Elliott handed it to him. It squawked loudly, and everyone winced. Dad apologized in a shaky voice and then cleared his throat. "Chloe's my only kid, and her mother died several years back. I suppose I'm here representing for both of us, but I've never been any good at this kind of thing. All I want to say is that I'm proud of you, honey. You found the one person who not only can handle you, but *wants* to handle you. And for your part, Ben, I like how you look at my daughter. I like what I see in you, and I'm proud to be able to call you son."

Elliott seemed to sense that my dad was growing a little emotional, so he retrieved the mic from my father's shaking hand. "We've put together a little slide show of these kids growing up. It'll play on a loop for you to enjoy during dinner. Please, enjoy the meal and the company."

The guests applauded briefly and then *awww*'d in unison as pictures of us as babies, as small kids, and as teenagers reeled through. I smiled at pictures of me in my mother's arms, wrestling with my father. I looked so *goofy*. In each of his photos, Bennett was well groomed and handsome, even in his awkward preteen years.

"Were you *ever* hideous?" I asked in a hiss. A picture of me came on screen and was met with loud laughter: it was the year of the worst haircut in the history of the world—jagged bangs, the rest of it basically a mullet— and braces so big I looked like I was eating train tracks.

"Wait for it," Bennett murmured.

Just after he said it, a picture came up of Bennett holding some sort of certificate. Clearly he'd had a growth spurt; his pants were too short, his hair was long and unkempt, and the picture caught him in the middle of a particularly unattractive laugh. He looked just a fraction less than gorgeous, but by no means hideous.

"I hate you," I said.

He leaned over, kissing the side of my head. "Sure you do."

The pictures ended in the present day, with a shot I recognized from the picture of us that Susan kept in the family room: Bennett stood with his arms behind me, bent and whispering something in my ear while I laughed. I leaned over, kissed my dad's cheek, then stood and hugged Elliott and Susan.

The pictures began to reel through again, and everyone began sipping at the wine the waiters poured into their glasses. I looked down our table, watching our wedding party in their unguarded moments. Sara said something under her breath as Max leaned close and kissed her cheek. Down the table, Will threw an almond at Hanna, and she tried to catch it with her mouth, missing by a mile. George and Julia argued about the ramifications of the return of acid wash. Bennett's niece Sofia crawled all over Henry's lap and Elliott poured water for Susan, who looked up at me and smiled, full of such happiness that I could practically see the entire history of Chloe and Bennett in her eyes, and how much she'd wanted this for her son. Beside me, Bennett reached under the table and slid his hand up my knee and under my skirt.

My heart squeezed so tight it felt like it stopped beating, and then took off in a heavy, stuttering gallop.

The rehearsal had been so disorganized that it wasn't until this moment, right here, that I felt the full force of our impending wedding.

I was getting married tomorrow.

To Bennett Ryan.

To the man who'd anger-fucked me into loving him.

I remembered . . .

"Miss Mills, it would make working with you so much easier if you wouldn't insist on ignoring all grammatical rules in your meeting minutes."

"Mr. Ryan, I noticed the company is offering communication training to entry-level managers. Shall I sign you up?"

"Take these invoices down to accounting. What, Miss Mills? Do you require a map?"

I reached for my water, hand shaking as I downed half of it.

"You okay, baby?" Bennett whispered in my ear. I nodded frantically, giving him the calmest smile I could manage. I'm sure I looked like a lunatic. I could feel sweat breaking out on my forehead, and my silverware clattered onto my bread plate as I fumbled for my napkin. Bennett stared in naked fascination, as if he were watching a lightning storm build in slow motion.

"It's nice to see you finally taking an interest in your physical fitness, Miss Mills."

Beautiful fucking Bastard.

"And then you're going to make up the hour lost this morning by doing a mock board presentation of the Papadakis account for me in the conference room at six."

And I remembered . . .

"Ask me to make you come. Say please, Miss Mills."

"Please go fuck yourself."

Bennett slid a calming hand along the back of my neck. I looked up at him, blinked rapidly. "I love you," I whispered, feeling like my heart was being strung up on a kite, sent headlong into the wind. It was nearly impossible to keep from climbing onto him, begging him to touch me.

"I love you, too." He leaned closer, brushed his lips across mine. All around us, people broke out in cheers and catcalls. But very carefully he pressed his mouth to my ear and murmured, "Don't you fucking tempt me right now, Mills. This isn't the place to test my willpower."

I tried to explain that I wasn't playing a game, I wasn't trying to seduce him right now, but no words came out.

He smiled, tucking a stray strand of hair behind my ear, but the sweet gesture was betrayed by his sharp hiss: "If you try to tease me with my father sitting right here, I'll take out any gentle tomorrow night and give you nothing but hard and fast. I'll leave you hungry and unsatisfied on our wedding night." He pulled back, winking, and then passed the basket of rolls to Elliott on his right.

I remembered when, during a meeting once, Henry had found the buttons to my ruined blouse on the floor of the conference room and Bennett had taunted me, asking me if they were indeed mine. *He'd* been the one to ruin the shirt, and there he'd been, acting blameless. I remembered the hurt, and the anger, and the terror I felt as I realized he was out to ruin my career in front of his family.

But he actually *hadn't* been. He was simply as fumbling as I was, trying to form a connection somehow, and completely at the mercy of this undeniable fire between us.

I'd run, livid, from the meeting as soon as it finished. The memory was so sharp in my thoughts, I could still hear the elevator doors close, feel the heat of his breath on my neck from all those months ago.

"Why are you suddenly so much more pissy than usual?" *he'd demanded.*

"It would be just like you to make me look like a career-climbing whore in front of your father."

"We're getting married tomorrow," I said on an exhale. "Right?"

"That's right." Bennett patted my hand, smiling indulgently at me, but I shook my head, reaching to grip his arm. My pulse spiked and I felt my hands grow clammy.

"I have the power? You're the one who pressed into my dick in the elevator. You're the one doing this to me."

"We're getting *married. Tomorrow.* Say it."

His smile faltered slightly, eyes searching mine, and he nodded. "We're getting married tomorrow."

I closed my eyes, remembering now how his expression had fallen wide open, his heart exposed to me for maybe the first time as I got myself off in his office. *"What are you doing to me?* he'd asked, almost bewildered.

"You okay there, Mills?" he whispered, glancing up and smiling tightly at a waiter when he put the first course down on the table in front of us.

"I don't want to walk out that door and lose what we found in this room."

I pushed my chair back, lurching away from the table and tripping down the row of seats, past our wedding party, and to the restrooms.

I ran upstairs and burst into the small side room reserved for the wedding party, set near the restrooms, and didn't even bother turning on the light. The room was small and stuffy; we'd kept the flowers in here earlier and the cloying perfume filled the dark space. I took gulping breaths, looking up at myself in the mirrors lining the entire span of the wall in front of me.

It was as if I could feel every emotion I'd ever experienced with Bennett, and all at once. Hate, lust, fear, regret, need, hunger, love,

love

love

blinding love.

I pulled at my necklace, feeling like I was being strangled with nostalgia, anticipation, and, above it all, need for it to be done, for us to make it official so fate couldn't suddenly decide to take a different path and somehow leave us enemies instead of lovers.

"Breathe, Chloe," I whispered.

The door opened and a slice of light cut into the space before it returned to darkness. Bennett's big, warm hands slid down my back and came to rest on my hips.

"Hey," he said, kissing the back of my neck, his deep voice spreading like a current across my skin.

I closed my eyes, straightening and turning into his arms. Pressing my face into his neck, I inhaled his after-shave, opened my mouth to suck hungrily on his skin. He felt like home, he tasted like home.

He groaned quietly, fingers digging into my sides, dragging up my back, *shaking*.

But with this reminder of the restraint he was making us both endure, a wave of anger and heat and frustration overtook me and I shoved at his chest, slamming my fists into him. "*You* did this to me! You and your stupid rule and your teasing smirk and the giant cock you won't share! Your long fingers and tongue that does that . . . that circle *thing*! You!" I gulped down a giant breath of air and continued, "You're such a perfect, shit-talking, stubborn, exacting, bossy *asshole*! And fuck you, Bennett! Why are you so damn smart and good at everything? Why do you love me? How did I get so lucky? You're turning me into a maniac! I thought I was going to start crying out there!"

He laughed silently and I could feel him shake his head next to me. "Unlikely. You cried a couple of years ago. I don't think you're due again until—"

I cut him off with a kiss, and I really had intended it to just be a firm, relieved kiss to shut him up—shut *myself* up—and thank him for being *him* when I needed it. But it went from playful to fevered as soon as he opened his mouth, let me slide my tongue over his bottom lip, and met me halfway with his.

With a growl, he had me lifted and pressed against the back wall, his hands sliding up the skirt of my dress, fingertips digging into my thighs. "You're not getting cold feet, are you?"

"No!" I gasped, my head falling back and hitting the wall heavily as he ground his cock between my legs.

"Because I'd drag you by your hair down that aisle."

I laughed, and it turned into a moan as his lips played their way up my neck and over my chin. "It's funny that you think you could drag me anywhere," I told him.

When he returned to me, I tilted my head away, pushing on his shoulders. "On your knees."

He glared at me. "Ex*cuse* me?"

"*Knees*," I repeated.

If looks could kill, I would be chopped up into tiny pieces and served with the calamari. But without speaking, Bennett lowered my feet to the floor before kneeling in front of me. He didn't require further instruction; he simply pulled one of my legs over his shoulders, leaned forward, and opened his mouth against my clit.

Bennett's only goal was to get me off, in record time. There was no teasing; there was no flicking of the tongue or gentle warm-up kisses around my soft, bare skin. There was only open mouth, suction and, finally, the press of his fingers at my entrance, swirling, gathering my slick lust with his fingertips.

But he didn't do what I expected. Instead, he slid his thumb into me and dragged his wet fingers to my backside, where he carefully pressed one just inside. I let out the most desperate, pathetic moan of my life and slid my hands into his hair, holding him steady so I could rock against his face. Bennett didn't penetrate me there often, but when he did it—whether with fingers or his cock—it always left me sated and dopey for days.

His mouth sucked and pulled at my tender skin, and his finger and thumb pressed together and away, a pulsing dark pleasure. The sensation was somehow both too much and not enough. I wanted everything he was doing to be deeper, and harder, and bigger almost to the point of pain. My pleasure built low in my belly, a steady, throbbing hum between my legs. I feared the explosion would elude me, that there was too much else happening out there, on the other side of the door. I worried nothing but Bennett's naked body would be enough, heavy and commanding, pounding into mine.

But then, as if reading my thoughts, he slid a second finger into my backside, and fucked me hard and fast until my thighs shook, my hands curled in his hair, and the growing sensation between my legs exploded into delicious flames that shot down my thighs and bowed my spine, tearing a cry from my throat.

Bennett didn't let up until I was gasping, clutching at

his shoulders and trying to push him away. Then, gently, he kissed my clit and leaned back, looking up at me.

"Think that will hold you over until tomorrow night?"

I let my head fall back against the wall, feeling like my legs were made of jelly. "Yeah."

"You look properly fucked."

Sighing, I mumbled, "I feel properly fucked. You and that magical mouth and those naughty fingers."

"Figured that might be in order." He stood, straightening his jacket with his other hand.

I reached down, cupping his cock, stroking down to his balls and back up, feeling the thick head of his erection. "One of us should get back out there. We've been gone . . . a few minutes. Seriously Bennett, that was pretty stunning."

I heard his teeth grind, and peeked up at him to see his tense jaw working side to side. "I know."

"So sorry I don't have time to reciprocate," I whispered, stretching to kiss his jaw.

"No you're not."

"Well," I said, patting his cheek, "you need to go wash up anyway. May as well pull double duty and jerk off in the bathroom." I kissed his chin, adding, *"Again."*

He bent low, inhaling into my neck, before slamming his hand on the wall beside my head, turning, and storming out of the dressing room. Walking to the wall, I flipped on the light and studied my reflection in the mirrors lining the room. I tucked a stray strand of hair back into my little diamond clip and smiled at myself in the mirror before stepping out into the hall.

Will walked out of the men's room just as Bennett shoved past him inside. Turning to me, he laughed, asking, "What's with him?"

Shrugging, I said simply, "It's his own fault."

He nodded in mock sympathy and then asked, "You ready for tomorrow?"

"Not remotely."

He put an arm around me. "It'll be perfect. And even if it's not perfect, there will be alcohol."

"I know," I said, smiling. "I'm actually not nervous, just—"

"Mommy, that's the man with the big weenis! I saw him in the bathroom earlier!"

We both looked down to see the small son of Bennett's third cousin Kate pointing at Will.

I slapped a hand over my mouth to hold in a loud burst of laughter. Will's hands flew up into the air and a look of horror passed over his face. "I swear I did *not* show him—"

"Oh, I know you didn't," Kate assured him, eyes wide and apologetic. She bit her lip, staring maybe a beat too long at Will. A long, uncomfortable silence passed before she seemed to remember herself and blinked down to her son. "He's potty training and my husband told me he was checking you out earlier." She did a full-body wince, adding, "Not that my *husband* was checking you out. And not that he wouldn't. Except, he wouldn't because he's married. And not into guys? But he did mention that our *son* was walking around and . . . Oh, God." Without another word, she grabbed her son's hand and pulled him into the women's room.

I blinked up to Will, eyes wide. "What was *that*?"

He shrugged, laughing a little. "The kid was walking around us at the urinals while his dad washed his hands. It wasn't a big deal."

"Why do women lose their ability to speak around you?"

"Do they now?" he asked, grinning flirtatiously at me. "*You're* speaking."

"That's because I'm more dragon than woman," I replied with a wink.

"Touché." Looking back at me, his eyes grew a little heated, as if he had a bone to pick with me. "There is something I want to discuss with you, however."

"William," I said, leaning against the wall, "I'm flattered, but if you're going to chastise me about something, you won't know what hit you when it's my turn to speak."

He exhaled, staring me down. "Honestly, Chloe, you're the one woman I'm sure would take me over her knee and break my spine. This is about your husband-to-be."

"What did he do now?"

Will exhaled slowly, eyes moving over my face. He was a worthy opponent, for sure. "I think you know what he did."

Looking over at him, I could see traces of lipstick on his cheeks, claw prints practically drawn through his hair. Will was the poker-faced, wisecracking brainiac seduction artist. It was actually a little fascinating to witness the cracks forming in his shell. "Oh, come on. Judy and Mary are kittens."

"Right," he said through a sharp laugh. "And I know Bennett put them up to this. I'm telling you, Chloe, that I'll behave myself for the rest of the weekend. I'll play along. But the second we're back from this wedding, and you've returned from your sexfest in Fiji, it's on. Do you understand?"

I gave him a thrilled smile, nodding enthusiastically.

"The psychotic clown I sent for his birthday will feel like a feather falling on a pillow atop a cloud. The laxative in my lunch? Child's play. If you think it was bad when I sent that fake resumé for his open assistant position and the stripper came for the interview? No. We're talking Defcon Five, *Vietcong*-level mind fucking, do you hear me, Chloe?"

"Can't wait, Dr. Sumner."

He pulled back, studying me. "It's a little unnerving how *excited* you look."

Straightening up, I pushed off the wall and patted his cheek. "I *am* excited. I like seeing that the only thing that will change after this week is that Bennett will have a ring on his finger and my last name after his first name. I like knowing that you guys will continue to escalate this big testicle war. You and Hanna will continue to be adorable and giddy, Max and Sara will continue to be disgustingly in love. Bennett will continue to alternately rock my world and make me insane. It's life as it should be."

As if on cue, Bennett stepped from the men's room, wearing an expression that told me he was much calmer. He gave me a little wink.

Will glared at him before turning and walking past us to head back downstairs to the party.

"Well?" I asked, when Bennett came close and bent to slide his lips across mine.

"Well, what?"

"Feel better?"

He shrugged. "Marginally."

"What was the fantasy?"

His hazel eyes grew heavy as he stared at my mouth. Leaning forward he murmured, "You were bound and gagged. I fucked you from behind, and didn't let you come."

When he kissed my cheek and pulled my hand to lead me back to our dinner, I knew he was telling me the absolute truth. And suddenly I didn't feel quite so sated anymore.

Dinner wound down and people began ordering cocktails, moving into small groups to talk, and venturing out onto the dance floor. From our table, Bennett and I sat watching. His long arm stretched out on the chair behind me, and he toyed with the ends of my hair.

"You're a pain in the ass," he said quietly.

"Well, you definitely weren't a pain in *mine*."

With a deep chuckle he whispered, "You're shameless."

"I am."

He shook his head next to me, reaching with his free hand for his drink.

I looked over to where Judith and Mary had Will sandwiched between them, grinding lewdly. "You're in trouble for that," I told Bennett. "Will said he's going 'Vietcong' on you."

"I figured."

Their hands moved up his sides, in his hair . . . seriously, he looked like he was in some AARP version of a Naughty by Nature video. He was trying to be a good sport, but, dear Lord, even the king of players could only do so much.

"You two troublemakers quit it now!" my dad yelled across the room.

"We're reminiscing, Freddy, relax!" Judith yelled back. When Judith not-so-discreetly reached down and grabbed Will's ass, he carefully pushed himself away, stumbling toward the DJ table and pulling the mic from the stand.

"Hanna!" The microphone squealed with feedback

and everyone slapped their hands over their ears. The DJ abruptly stopped the music, and silence roared through the room. Will seemed completely unfazed. "Hanna. Look at me."

We turned to look at her where she stood across the room, talking to Mina. Her eyes had gone wide, and she shook her head slightly at him. "Oh, God," she whispered.

"Remember that thing I alluded to on the plane?" he asked, eyes glued to her.

A tiny smile played at her lips. "Jog my memory, Player Will."

He squeezed his eyes closed, took a deep breath before looking back at her, and said, "Marry me?"

I was clearly not the only person to gasp. It felt like the entire room did it in unison. As if anticipating my needs, Bennett reached into his pocket and handed me a handkerchief. Across the room, I saw Max do the same thing for Sara. But whereas she took it and thanked him, I batted Bennett's hand away.

"Sorry, Chloe," Will said, looking as though he wasn't even sure he was awake and doing this in front of fifty people. "I realize my timing sucks."

"Don't you dare interrupt this moment to talk to me!" I called out, gesturing wildly to Hanna across the room. "Keep going! This is the best thing to happen so far tonight."

Bennett dug his fingers into my shoulder, laughing darkly next to me. "You're in trouble for that."

Hanna took a few steps closer and the dance floor between her and Will cleared. "Are you asking me this because you're afraid of the handsy cougars on the dance floor?"

"A little," Will admitted, nodding frantically. He swallowed thickly and repeated in a squeak, "A little. But I've wanted to ask every day, and every day I get scared." Holding up his hand before she could misinterpret his words, he hastily added, "Not because I'm not sure. But because I want you to be as sure as I am."

I watched as Hanna walked across the room, took the mic from Will's shaking hand, put it back into the stand, and stretched to kiss him before saying something that none of us heard, but that made Will Sumner smile more widely than I'd ever seen him smile.

The guests broke out in roaring cheers and Bennett signaled to the caterer to bring trays of champagne around. Music pulsed, heavy and wild from the speakers, and the dance floor quickly grew packed with bodies.

Bennett stood and looked down at me. "Let's go dance, Almost–Mrs. Ryan."

"Only if you let me lead, Almost–Mr. Mills."

CHAPTER SIX

"So was it the two mai tais I drank," Chloe began, "or did Will really propose to Hanna tonight?"

"He did," I said, turning off the water. "In the middle of our rehearsal dinner. With a *microphone*. In front of both my family and yours, and probably loud enough that the entire restaurant upstairs heard him. Rumor has it she said *yes*."

"Okay then," she said around her toothbrush, bending to rinse her mouth. I watched her bend, her ass push out suggestively, and felt my pulse hum heavy in my chest, the weight of need curling deep in my stomach.

"You should hurry up," I said, tossing the towel to the sink and leaning against the counter.

"Are we going somewhere?" She stood, facing me in her tiny lace slip, eyes wide and mock-innocent, as if she wasn't the same woman who'd just made me go down on her in a dressing room while our wedding party and family drank and dined obliviously downstairs. I was glad she was finally my Chloe again, the woman who was every bit as greedy as I was.

But now it was my turn.

"No. You're going to suck my dick and then I'm going to fuck you until someone has to bang on the door and tell us it's time to get married," I said, unbuttoning my shirt.

She straightened, eyes tracking each inch of skin as it became visible. "Oh?"

I pushed her against the wall, ran my hands down her curves to rest on her ass. "You may have visible trouble walking tomorrow."

"And your rule?"

"Rules are for suckers and idiots who aren't getting laid." Leaning in, I ran my tongue along her neck, bent to lift her and wrap her legs around my waist. I walked us into the bedroom, shutting off the lights as we went. "And I am tired of being a sucker, Miss Mills."

"Did you come to this conclusion before or after you made me come?" she asked, then gasped when I tossed her to the mattress.

"Why are you still talking?" I growled against her mouth. I kissed her hard and with all the frustration I'd felt the past week. I sucked in her little sounds, hissed as her fingers pushed my shirt from my body and she forced my pants down with her legs.

"You will suck me off," I said. "And then I'm going to fuck you on your hands and knees." My head snapped up at a sound from the other room, and I pulled back, blinking into the darkness. "Did you hear that?" I asked, almost certain I heard footsteps across the tile floor in the foyer.

"Fuck yes," she sighed, oblivious, still dragging her nails down my sides. "Tell me what else—"

"*Chloe—*"

"Close, but not quite, sweet stuff," a male voice said next to my ear.

I bolted upright into a fight stance, heart racing just as the lights flipped on.

"Jesus, George. We said to knock!" a woman hissed.

I scrambled to hide Chloe's mostly naked body. *"Mina?"* I said, wincing and mostly blind from the sudden light as the shape of my sister-in-law stepped into the room.

Someone threw a shirt at me, but it was quickly batted away.

"Don't you dare!" George warned, rushing to stand in front of me. "I will personally throttle anyone who hands this man a single piece of clothing. And, damnit, Mina. You said he'd be naked."

"Oh, my bad," she said, smiling. "I forgot he's guarding his virtue and trying to keep it pure before the wedding. I might have forgotten to tell you that. Though judging by the looks of things," she dropped her eyes to my boxers, "he was about to give it up. Might want to put something over that, Ben. Mommy's coming."

I suddenly realized I was standing in only my boxers. *Hard.*

"Get out!" I said, reaching for a pillow and holding it in front of me. Chloe bent to the floor and pulled on a cotton robe. The intruders were dressed in black from head to toe and looked like a group of cartoon banditos. I'm sure that at any *other* moment I would have found this hilarious.

"Oh calm down, Bennett," my mother said, walking into the room with Sara and Julia right on her heels. "We're here to take Chloe with us."

"*What?* How did you people even get a key?" I asked.

"You do *not* want to know," George said.

Mom rounded the bed and reached for Chloe's hand. "You know the rule, Bennett: groom can't see the bride the day of the wedding. And we are exactly five minutes from that." She leaned close to me, whispering, "I texted you earlier to warn you we'd be sneaking in and stealing her."

"*Mom!*" I yelled, losing patience. "I don't have time to read five hundred text messages a day about Dad's pants and the A/C in your room and your favorite dish at the restaurant downstairs!"

"Does anyone care what *I* think?" Chloe asked.

"No," George and Mina said in unison.

"Fine," she said, tightening her robe. "You're all lucky I'm exhausted and got some earlier or I'd kick every one of your asses. Just get me to a bed. I don't even care whose. It can be yours for all I care," she said, pointing to George.

"Not a chance in hell, princess."

Had the world gone completely insane?

"Sara," I said, spinning to face her, pleading. "How did they talk you into this? You're supposed to be the nice one. They will drag you down with them, Dillon—run."

She shrugged. "This is actually kind of fun. I mean, with

your newfound chastity we expected to find you crocheting or playing Scrabble or something. This is way better."

"You're all nuts," I said. "All of you. Even my mother."

"Two minutes!" George called out. The room broke into a flurry of activity: drawers were opened and rummaged through; the armoire was searched for anything that might be needed tomorrow. The bathroom was ransacked and pilfered of every single one of Chloe's things.

"Oh stop being such a tight-ass, Bennett. It's tradition, and tomorrow when you see her walk down the aisle it will all be worth it. Do we have everything?" Mom called.

Several different voices confirmed that indeed, everything was in order for the kidnapping of my fiancée, and after a mad flurry of activity in the main room, Chloe was hustled out without so much as a lingering kiss on my lips, and the suite fell deadly quiet.

It took me hours to finally fall asleep. The room was too quiet, the bed too empty, and I hadn't gotten laid. Again. My hand was starting to feel like a pity fuck.

Waking up alone sucked. One would think I'd be accustomed to it by now—with our busy schedules one of us was always coming or going and we each spent our fair share of nights in an empty bed—but now that I'd grown accustomed to waking with Chloe warm and pliable and *right there,* it felt wrong, like a vital part of me was missing.

It was still dark; early enough that a damp chill hung in

the air and the birds were relatively quiet. With the stillness outside, the ocean seemed louder than ever. I was hard and alone, and Chloe was somewhere nearby, but too fucking far away to touch. My stomach twisted and I closed my eyes, reaching for a pillow to block it all out.

This was going to be a long day.

I forced myself up, moved to the bathroom to take care of business, shower, and dress. We were getting married today. *Married.* And the mental list in my head of everything that needed to be done was about as long as the hours remaining in the day.

There were too many clocks here, I'd decided. There was the one I wore, which Chloe got me the day we opened the New York office of RMG. An ornate clock over the wet bar, one on the TV, another on the docking station by the bed. I could tell from almost any point in the suite exactly how many hours until Chloe would be awake, until I got to see her again, until she was my wife.

———

Will and Max were waiting for me downstairs. Huddled together near the fireplace in the grand room, they were bickering over a map displayed on Max's phone.

"It's on University," Will was saying.

"It's not," Max argued. "It's the one on Robinson." He looked up, took in my giant scowl, and shook his head. "Good morning, sunshine. I'm assuming we didn't sleep well last night?"

I rolled my eyes. "You would know. Were you missing a very pregnant girlfriend? Because she ended up in my room."

"What?" Will said.

"The entire bridal party *including* George showed up last night, intent on stealing my fiancée so I wouldn't see her until the ceremony. I'm assuming they've got her bound and gagged in this hotel somewhere while they cover her in white lace and iridescent sparkles." I took in Will's posture, the circles under his eyes, and his nonstop yawning. "What's up with you?"

"Hanna," he said, stifling another yawn. "Not sure if it's the cougar sisters or what but damn, I haven't gotten a full night's sleep since we got here."

"I hate you both," I said with a sweeping hand gesture.

"Good to see you're in such high spirits today, mate," Max laughed.

"Suck it, Stella," I said, breezing by him and heading in the direction of the concierge desk. He and Will moved into step on either side of me.

The concierge looked up as we approached. I gave her my name and handed over my identification and credit card, and waited while she finished the rental paperwork. I'd reserved a large cargo van for our trip to the cleaner; wanting to make sure everything would arrive in perfect condition, even the garment bags pristine. I closed my hand around the keys, feeling a sense of calm at finally being in control of *something.* This was how you got things done: you fucking did them yourself.

"Mr. Ryan!"

I turned at the sound of my name, the familiar clicking of heels on the wood floor.

Shit.

"Kristin," I said. "We were just on our way out."

"The clothes," she said, nodding toward the key ring in my hand.

"Is there something I can do for you?"

"Ahhh," she started, and gave me the most pained smile I'd ever seen. My stomach dropped on instinct. "There's a slight issue."

Deep breaths.

"'Slight'?" I repeated. *Small accident. Tiny problem. Minor wrinkle.*

"Small," she assured me with a smile. "Insignificant."

"Here we go," I heard Will say.

We followed her out a back door, across a patio, and down to the lawn where they were currently setting up for the wedding. Or trying to. My shoe sank into the grass with a sickening squelch on the first step.

"Oh, God," I said, looking around. *"Fuuuuck."* The entire area was flooded. Chairs were knocked over, tables askew with legs sinking into the swampy grass, workers rushing around in a panic.

"A sprinkler line broke during the night," she said, apologetically. "They've stopped the water but as you can see . . ."

"Wow," Will said, poking at a puddle with the tip of his sneaker.

I scrubbed my face with my hands and felt Max grip my shoulder, squeezing.

"They can fix it though, yeah?" he said, realizing I was two seconds from losing it and stepping in front of me.

"Oh, definitely," Kristin was saying, though I couldn't be sure through the sound of blood whooshing in my ears.

My phone buzzed in my pocket and I pulled it out, panicked that Chloe had seen this and was freaking out.

But it was only my mother: Honey, do you happen to know if your father packed his black dress shoes? I can't find them in our room but he says he did.

I shoved the phone back in my pocket, tuning in as Kristin was saying, "They've fixed the line, now we'll work on getting this area dried up or move everything a bit farther down the beach."

Max turned to me, charming smile in place. "See? Nothing to worry about, mate. We'll pick up the dresses, get you some food . . . or maybe some alcohol, judging by your expression, and everything will be fine when we return. And if it's all the same to you, I'll just be taking these." He plucked the keys from my hand.

"What are you doing?" I asked, reaching for them.

"Sorry, Ben, best for everyone, I'm afraid. You're likely to mow down pedestrians in your state of mind and that would put a definite wrinkle in the wedding festivities."

"I can drive, Max. Give me the goddamn keys."

"Have you seen yourself? Got that vein thing happening,"

he said, reaching up to tap my forehead before I smacked his hand away.

Will snorted behind me and I turned, leveling him with a glare. He held his hands out in front of him. "The man has a point," he said, backing away.

I spun to Max again. "Do you even know how to drive?"

"Of course I do."

"*Here?*"

He waved me off. "Left side, right side. How different can it be?"

———

Max guided us back through the hotel and out to valet. We argued the entire way, me calling Max a bossy asshole, and Max asking me where I'd left my purse. Will trailed behind, half asleep on his feet.

An attendant approached us immediately, ignoring our bickering as he matched the keys to a list pinned to a clipboard. We followed him to a white cargo van parked at the curb, cool in the shade of a grouping of palms. I waved off his offer of directions, placed a few dollars in his hand, and turned my back as he walked away.

"So, the plan. Will," Max said, waiting a beat before reaching out and smacking Will across the cheek.

Will startled, eyes wide. "What?"

"You all right?"

"God, I'm just *so* fucking tired."

"Well, have some coffee and snap out of it," Max said. "You'll ride with us to the cleaners, then take a cab from there to pick up the rings."

"What, am I your little sidekick now? Why can't Henry help with any of this?"

"Because Henry talks too much and you're much prettier," Max said. "Who knows? We may need to sweet talk a feisty old bird at the dry cleaners, and who is better than you at seducing cougars?" He patted Will's cheek, cooing, "No one, Blossom. No one."

Will yawned, clearly too tired to argue, and waved him off. "Yeah, whatever."

Max walked around the van, stopping just beside the passenger door. "Ben, your chariot awaits."

"Fuck you," I said, slugging him in the shoulder as I climbed into the seat.

But I could hear him laughing as he rounded the front and got in, asking, "All right back there, William?"

"Yeah, yeah," came the mumbled reply. "You're both assholes."

Max put the keys in the ignition and the engine roared to life. After grinning proudly at me he turned back and his face grew puzzled when he attempted to put the van in gear, only to be met with a horrible grinding noise.

"That's encouraging," I said.

"Would you stop being such a twat and relax? I've got this."

"Of course you do."

The van lurched forward and I made a dramatic point about fastening my seat belt. The tires screeched as we took the first turn and I reached blindly for the dash, anything to hold on to. Will wasn't as lucky, and the sound of him tumbling around in the cargo area could be heard from the front seat.

"When was the last time you actually drove a car?" I asked, bracing myself as we prepared to take another turn.

He pursed his lips as he considered this. "Vegas," he said with a nod, completely unfazed by the trail of blaring horns in our wake.

"Vegas? I don't remember you driving anywhere in Vegas."

He checked the directions on his phone, blazed through a yellow light at the very last minute, and nearly rear-ended a car at a stop sign. "It's possible I borrowed a car while you boys were occupied."

"*Borrowed? Jesus.*"

"Yeah. And actually . . . to be fair, it was a limo, not a car. But that's not the point. I got there safe and sound in the end."

"And did you notice anything unusual? Maybe a few rude hand gestures aimed in your direction? Police sirens?"

After several near-misses with much smaller cars—because you could practically see the Brit working to flip left and right around in his mind—we pulled up in front of the cleaners. Max glared at me as he put the van in park.

"Oh, God, somebody let me out," Will groaned. I climbed down and opened the back door, watching as Will stumbled from the cargo area, and immediately moved to throw up in the bushes. Apparently, my point had been made.

The dry cleaner was a small, nondescript business nestled between a Chinese food restaurant and a comic book store in the center of a strip mall. Max motioned for me to lead the way and we paused at the front door, gazing up at a neon sign reading *Satisfaction Guaranteed* buzzing overhead.

"Bit unfortunate, that," Max mused under his breath.

Thank God the clothes were ready. We opened each bag to make sure everything was accounted for—six dresses, eight tuxedos—and proceeded to carry them out to the van. Max made sure to keep his promise to my mother, and kept me far from Chloe's wedding gown.

"There's no way you're driving us back," I said to Max once the last bag had been loaded.

"You still going on about that?" he asked

"Did you see yourself out there? After he *puked,* Will was practically kissing the ground." I reached for the keys, managing to snag them from his hand.

"Like you could do any better? My gran's a better driver than you. She's eighty-two and has *glaucoma.*"

"I'm sorry, I couldn't hear you over the sound of the police helicopter and the warrant for your arrest," I said, and swore as Max grabbed the keys back from me.

Will stepped between us, snagging the key ring and rubbing his temples. "Will you two just shut the fuck up? If I have to go back to the hotel and run from those women all night, I am not putting up with your bullshit, too. Ben? You drive," he said, pushing the keys into my hand again. "Max? Play nice and wait your turn. My cab is here. I'll pick up the rings and meet you back there." He looked between us, waiting for some sort of protest.

"Yeah," I said.

"Fine," Max sighed.

"Good. Now try not to kill each other on the way back."

———

I entered the address for the Del into my phone and waited for the directions to appear. Max sat silently in the seat next to me.

"Thanks," I said, and started the engine. Although we'd barely made it to the dry cleaner's alive, Max had handled the entire morning with his trademark calm and optimism. I had to admit I'd be drunk and firing employees that weren't even mine in the hotel lobby if he hadn't stepped in and taken charge.

"You're a dick," he said back. I smiled as I pulled out of the parking lot.

Saturday afternoon in San Diego meant traffic, a lot of it. We'd been lucky enough on the way in, but it had definitely picked up by the time we pulled on the freeway. Max was insisting I was going the wrong way when his phone rang.

"Yeah, Will," he said, and then paused before putting it on speaker. "Go ahead."

"Which one of you two idiots was supposed to close the van door?"

"What?" I asked, and then looked up to the rearview mirror. Sure enough, one of them had been left open and was swinging back and forth on its hinges.

"Fuck!" I shouted, and it was as if the world suddenly shifted into high speed. Cars appeared out of nowhere, veering, honking, tires squealing past us as I tried to make my way to the side of the road. In the rearview mirror I saw the breeze catch the edge of one of the bags, curling it like it weighed no more than a candy wrapper. Up and back down. Up and back down. Max fumbled with his seat belt before vaulting to the back, arms outstretched as he reached for the endangered garment. But it was too late. We hit a small bump and it was just enough for the wind to lift the entire stack, letting them hover in midair before they were gone, sliding like dominoes out the door and onto the asphalt below.

It was pandemonium. I swore. I cut off a huge truck as I veered into the far right lane and came to a skidding stop at the side of the freeway. I wrenched open my door, shouting for Max as we both jumped out, watching in horror as cars flew down the two-lane highway, the garment bags scattered along it.

"Over there!" I yelled, spotting the larger of the bags near the median, the one that contained Chloe's dress.

Will's cab came to a screeching halt just behind us and we split up, each of us moving in opposite directions, sprinting and dodging through traffic to scoop up the dresses one by one and drag them back to the side of the road.

Cars honked all around us and the air filled with the pungent scent of tires skidding on asphalt. Above it all my pulse hammered in my ears, and my only thought was to get to Chloe's dress and bring it back. I tried to avoid thinking about what failure would mean.

I ignored a particularly angry string of curse words shouted at me from a Benz and managed to make it to the median in one piece. I looked at Chloe's bag, frantically searching the exterior for any damage. It seemed fine, intact except for a small rip on the bottom edge.

I made it back to the van and pushed it into Max's arms. "Check her dress," I said, bending at the knees and filling my lungs with oxygen, praying to God that her wedding gown was okay.

"It's fine," Max said, the relief in his voice clear even above the roar of passing traffic. "Perfect."

I let out a breath. "Thank fuck. Do we have them all?" I walked over to the van to see how many remained inside.

Will looked down to the garments in his arms. "Four," he said.

"Six," Max counted, panting.

"There's four back here," I said. "How many were there again?"

"Fourteen. All of us, Henry, the ring bearer, your dad, Chloe's dad, Chloe, the girls, George, your mom, and the flower girl. Right?" Will asked, counting down on his fingers, still hunched on the asphalt.

I nodded. "Let's get the fuck out of here."

This time, nobody fought over who got to drive.

———

I felt like I'd run a marathon by the time we got back to the hotel. We pulled up to valet and Kristin met us at the curb, ready to take over from there. She assured me that the worst of the water had been dealt with, and asked if I wanted to see how the preparations were coming. I declined, wanting nothing more than a shower, a nap, and for it to be time to meet Chloe at the altar. I looked down at my watch: three hours to go.

Will pulled up as we stood there, paid his driver, and stepped out of the cab. He held up his arm to show us the bright blue bag swinging from his fingertips.

"The rings are here," Max said, bumping my shoulder with his. "Makes it feel a bit more official, wouldn't you agree?"

I nodded, too relieved to even mock Will for his stupid swagger.

"Well, look who's the only one that hasn't fucked anything up today—" he said just as his toe caught a crack in the concrete and he pitched forward, crashing to the ground. The bag flew from his hands, the boxes flew from the bag, and of course, my newly polished ring tumbled out and onto the driveway.

I'm not sure who dove onto the asphalt first, but in the end it was Max holding out my wedding band, a deep dent in the strip of platinum running through the center. I was annoyed, sure, but after the day I'd had, it seemed a perfect reminder for the rest of my life: Remember that time you almost ruined your wife's wedding dress? Better to feel that dent, I suppose, than her wrath for the next sixty years.

"Doesn't look too bad," Max was saying. He placed it on his finger, straightened his hand out in front of him. "Can hardly see it, really."

We all nodded.

"Know what would make it completely go away?" Will said.

"What's that, William?" Max asked.

His answer was simple: "Alcohol."

I didn't get *completely* shitfaced. It was my wedding day, after all. But after a couple of drinks with the boys, I felt better than I had all week. And I was ready to get this fucking show on the road.

It was strange to get ready alone. Showering, shaving, dressing in the empty suite. For any other big event, Chloe would be by my side, happily chatting about whatever was on her mind. But for the biggest event of our lives—our wedding—I was preparing solo. I'd put on a tuxedo dozens of times in my life, eventually getting so comfortable wearing them that I barely glanced at my reflection before leaving the house. But here, as I stared back at myself, I was aware that Chloe would look down the aisle at me, walk toward me, agree to marry me. I wanted to be exactly what she'd always pictured her husband would be. I tried to straighten my hair with my fingers, made sure I hadn't missed a spot shaving. I checked my mouth for any stray toothpaste, tugged at my shirt cuffs.

For the first time all week, I was the one texting my mother.

Any doubts I'd had about Kristin were gone the moment I stepped outside and saw the ceremony setup. Rows of white chairs draped in sheer white and Tiffany blue ribbon stretched in front of me; white flower petals covered the aisle. A sea of tables draped in crystal and silver and more Tiffany blue covered the lawn area. Chloe's favorite flowers—orchids—were everywhere: in vases, clinging to the branches of huge potted trees, hanging in fragrant clusters from the tent ceilings. The sun was just starting to set, the guests were all seated, and I stole a moment to steady myself, gripping Henry's shoulder as I took it all in.

Kristin motioned that it was time to begin and I nodded, vaguely aware of the soothing music and the unbelievable sunset and the *huge fucking moment* in front of me. I reached for my mom's arm and began escorting her down the aisle.

"Did you ask the caterer if they got fresh—"

"Not now, Mom," I hissed through clenched teeth, smiling at the guests.

"You okay, sweetheart?" she asked when we reached her seat and I kissed her cheek.

"Almost." I kissed her one more time, and took my place at the end of the aisle, my heart clawing its way up my throat.

The music began and Sara and Henry were the first down the aisle. Even from where I stood, I could see she looked absolutely stunning. Her smile was huge, and she seemed to be almost laughing as she moved toward me. The first thing I noticed was the soft sound of suction as the heel of her shoe sank into the wet ground with each step. I exhaled a steadying breath, knowing it could have been much, *much* worse. And Sara *was* laughing. Surely, this was a good sign?

The second thing I noticed was the low hum of giggles that began near the back rows of seating, and grew louder as Sara and my brother moved toward me. I looked to Henry, who seemed to be barely holding it together, and then back to Sara, narrowing my eyes and I took in the full length of her body.

Oh

my

God.

A wide set of greasy tire tracks cut across her dress where it covered her very round and very pregnant stomach.

I was gripped by a white-hot rush of panic as I remembered the dresses, the way they'd looked scattered like roadkill as traffic whizzed by all around them. Sara looked like she and her baby had been run over by a truck. I felt all of the blood drain from my face.

"Oh, no," I groaned. All I'd cared about was the state of Chloe's dress. We hadn't even thought to look at the others.

As if Sara read my mind, she shook her head and motioned behind her, mouthing the words *she's perfect,* in reassurance.

I closed my eyes for a beat, urging myself to relax. *Chloe is fine. She's not going to come down the aisle with a cleaver. Just fucking calm down, Ben.*

The music changed and I heard the sound of three hundred and fifty bodies stand up, a collective sigh that ran through the guests. I opened my eyes just as everyone turned to see the bride at the end of the aisle.

My Chloe.

Everything seemed to settle at once and for the first time in my life, absolutely nothing else mattered. Not deadlines or work, just *this.* My brain—which thrived on spreadsheets and order and managing every detail of my life *and* the lives of those around me—had gone quiet. Not in an unpleasant way, but in a way that finally said, *take a seat and pay attention because this moment is bigger than you and every decision you've ever made.*

Chloe's chin was tucked low, her arm looped through her dad's and she clutched a bouquet of orchids in her free hand. Her hair was piled on top of her head and where I'd normally be plotting how I'd get it down and get my fingers in it while I threw her down onto any available flat surface, all I could think about was how I wanted to leave it up. I could see every inch of her face, and she looked so beautiful. I wanted to freeze this moment, stretch it out, and make it last forever.

It was clear that Chloe, even down to the last moment, was working something out. Her eyes were closed, her face arranged in a look of concentration as she sifted through her thoughts. Just as clear was the moment she figured it all out. Lifting her head, her eyes moved up the aisle to me, and it was as if time stopped and everything else fell away. I could feel myself smile, then see it reflected in the way her entire face seemed to light up, and I did the only thing I could think.

I whispered the words, "Come here."

Chapter Seven

Breathe in.

Breathe out.

It's only three hundred and fifty people looking at me.

It's only a river of mud on the aisle.

It's only a tire print across my maid of honor's pregnant belly.

It's only one ceremony, it's only getting through one day. It's only the love of your life at the end of that aisle.

My father tucked my arm into the crook of his, and wrapped his fingers over mine. "Ready, sweetheart?"

I swallowed, nodding, and said, "No."

"You have second thoughts over marrying this Benson character?"

I looked up at him and laughed at the teasing in his eyes. "No, I don't have any second thoughts over *Benson*. It's just . . . the way the last two days have gone, I'm worried there will be an earthquake when I walk down the aisle, or a tsunami, or—"

"Well, maybe there will be an earthquake, or maybe

there will be a tsunami. But you can't control the elements any more than you can control who you love. So are we going to do this wedding business or go get a drink in a bunker?"

I squeezed his hand and took a step forward, moving from the solid concrete of the patio to the soft, sodden mess of the lawn. My foot sank into the grass, and I pulled it up with a loud squelching sound. Beside me, my father nearly lost his balance in the mud.

"Pretend you're a feather," Dad whispered, and we both broke into laughter. "Lighter than air."

But then we turned the slight corner and I saw it.

The guests.

The wedding party.

The man who was going to be my husband in only a matter of minutes.

His eyes met mine and the biggest smile I'd ever seen stretched across his face. For several long seconds, I couldn't walk. I could barely *breathe*. The only thing I could do was stare at Bennett standing at the end of the aisle, waiting for me. He wore a perfectly tailored tux, and a perfectly devastating smile. He looked just like I felt: elated, overwhelmed, on the verge of falling over.

I saw his mouth say the words *Come here*.

And suddenly I couldn't get to him fast enough. I pulled my father forward, ignoring his quiet chuckle at my haste, ignoring the wet suction of the mud as it slipped into my shoe, ignoring the fact that I was moving faster than we'd rehearsed and the song wouldn't get to the right point by the time I reached the altar. I didn't care. I wanted to get to Bennett, put my hands in his, rush through the vows, and get to the "I do" as soon as humanly possible.

I bent, pulling my muddy sandals from my feet. Tossing them to the side, I ignored the loud splat they made in a puddle and hitched my dress above my ankles. I smiled when the crowd laughed and broke into applause, and I pulled my dad faster down the aisle, practically running. He stopped me up short halfway there, at the border of where the grass met the sand.

"This is the perfect metaphor," Dad said quietly, kissing my nose. "I got you halfway there, sweetheart; you do the rest." He kissed my cheek and then released me to run full bore the rest of the way down the petal-strewn sand and hurl myself into Bennett's waiting arms.

Cameras clicked all around us, and the guests were yelling their approval as Bennett swung me in a small, slow circle, my face in his neck and his mouth open and pressed to my shoulder.

I could imagine how we looked: not even married yet, clutching each other as if our lives depended on it, my feet exposed as Bennett spun me, the bottoms dark with mud and stark against the perfect white of my gown.

Carefully, carefully he put me down and beamed down at me. "Hey."

I swallowed back a sound that would probably have

come out somewhere between a cry and a gasp and said, "Hey yourself."

We hadn't seen each other since I'd been kidnapped from the room just as we were about to attack each other, and I could see it in his eyes: he wanted to kiss me. He wanted to kiss me with such hunger that it made us both vibrate, stare at each other's mouths, lick our lips in unison.

Soon, I mouthed.

He gave me a tiny nod, and we turned together to face the officiant, the Honorable James Marsters, who appeared completely baffled.

He leaned closer, whispering, "Have we finished the ceremony?" His watery blue eyes swam with confusion, and he peeked down at his notes before looking back at us.

With the sweetness of his expression and the perfect timing of this question, I bit my lip to keep from laughing out loud. Bennett slid his amused eyes to me and then back to the man before us.

"No, Judge. I apologize . . . my wife-to-be and I got a little carried away with our greeting." He tilted his head and murmured, "Neither the first nor the last time, actually."

"At least we know what we're getting into," I said, and beside me Sara laughed. I handed her my bouquet and turned to face Bennett as he took hold of my hands.

And once I was up there with him, I wanted to savor

every second. The judge read through his opening read-
ings about love, and marriage. I absorbed every word,
somehow, while still being completely lost in the intensity
of Bennett's expression.

As I recited my vows, I felt him shift closer, relished
the warm hum of his skin pressed to mine where our
hands met.

When it was his turn, I watched his lips as he repeated
every single vow:

I promise to be your lover and friend . . .

Your ally in conflict and your accomplice in mischief . . .

Your greatest fan and your toughest adversary . . .

His eyes twinkled and he tickled the palm of my hand
with the pad of his thumb when he said this, and then, very
slowly, he looked down at my mouth and licked his lips.

The bastard.

His eyes darkened and his voice lower when he repeated, *I promise to be faithful, loyal, and put your needs
above all others . . . this is my vow to you, Chloe, my only
lover and my equal in all things.*

Suddenly my dress felt cinched too tight. The breeze
off the water seemed too weak.

The officiant turned to me and asked, "Chloe, do you
take this man to be your lawfully wedded husband? To
honor and cherish him, to have and to hold from this day
forward, for better, for worse, for richer, for poorer, in
sickness and in health, to love and cherish always?"

The first time I tried to push the words out, they got stuck beneath the weight of emotion in my throat. Finally, I managed, "I do."

He turned and asked Bennett the same thing, and without hesitation, Bennett's deep voice easily carried the two life-altering syllables: "I do."

We each turned, he to Henry, and I to Sara, to retrieve our wedding rings. And as the judge spoke to us about the meaning of the rings, and I slid Bennett's onto his finger, the only thing I could feel was the brilliance of Bennett's smile as he stared down at it.

Damn, that ring looked good on his finger. This man was officially *mine*. If I couldn't get my face tattooed on his arm, this ring would be a nice consolation prize. I moved my fingertip over his, feeling the smooth metal on his skin, but he pulled back a little, resisting my touch as his eyes went wide, just as my finger made contact with an enormous scratch in the platinum.

I pulled his hand up to look closer. What the fuck? Was there an actual *dent* in his wedding ring?

When I looked up at his face again, he shook his head slightly. "It's okay," he whispered.

"What the hell is this?" I asked under my breath.

"I'll explain later," he hissed.

I felt the fire in my gaze and he barely contained his laugh as the judge called out, "If there is anyone present who has reason to oppose the marriage of this man to this woman, please speak now or forever hold your peace."

The guests grew completely quiet, and I stood, staring up at Bennett for a beat until the loud, deafening blast of a ship's horn ripped through the silence. I clapped my hands over my ears, and the entire wedding party jumped and ducked in surprise. Several people screamed. The sound seemed to linger, reverberating across the sand and up over the lawn before being swallowed by the hulking mass of the hotel.

"Well," Bennett said, smiling, "I guess we couldn't move forward without the universe at least giving us a fair warning."

At that, everyone erupted into laughter and applause, and with an enormous smile, the judge proclaimed, "Very well then. By the power vested in me by the state of California, I now pronounce you *husband* and wife. Chloe, you may kiss your groom."

I did a little dance at this small victory. Bennett gave a little growl of defeat but then leaned into me as I stepped on my toes, shoeless and inches shorter than my husband—*my husband!*—and pulled him down to me.

I didn't care that there were people watching.

I didn't care that the expectation was that we would give a small kiss now and enjoy many more, deeper kisses later.

Right now, as of this moment, this man was my fucking *husband,* and I needed to make sure everything felt the same.

I relished the way his arms tightened around me so

intensely I lost my breath. I relished the firm press of his mouth on mine, and the parting of his lips, the gentle slide of his tongue across mine . . . once, twice, three times, and the last time just a little deeper until I could feel the vibration of his sounds and practically *taste* his urgency. His breaths came out shallow and uneven on my tongue and his quiet words—*ah, fuck, Chlo,* and *need to get you alone*—finally made me pull away before I started stripping off his tux right here at the altar.

Breathless and grinning like idiots, we turned and faced a lawn-full of guests with hands suspended in the air, prepared to clap but wearing expressions of shock frozen on their faces.

Apparently we'd been a little wild in our first kiss as husband and wife.

"Go on girl, get yours!" George shouted, just as Judith yelled, "Now that's how you kiss a woman!" breaking the spell and the whole group in front of us broke into roaring applause.

"Ladies and gentlemen," the judge shouted above the mayhem. "It is my pleasure to introduce Bennett and Chloe Ryan!"

Chloe Ryan?

I turned and had just aimed my harshest glare at Bennett and his widening grin when chaos erupted all around us. Sara's arms swallowed me, and then Julia's and George's and Mina's. I felt my father's hands on my face and his giant smooch to my cheek. I was hugged by Elliott and Susan in tandem, lifted by Henry and Max in turn, kissed on the cheek by Will, and then I felt Bennett's smooth, warm hand wrapping around my arm and pulling me with him down the aisle, away from the tight press of the wedding party.

We ran, tripping through the mud, leaving wet footprints all along the patio. Inside, Bennett pulled me into the kitchen, where the caterers stopped what they were doing; the clattering of pots and dishes, the roaring of commands and replies went completely silent as Bennett turned and slammed me into the wall, his mouth on my neck, my jaw, my ears, my lips. He ran a hand up my side, gripping my breast through my wedding dress and I felt him begin to harden against my stomach.

"Tonight," he growled, returning to my neck. "Tonight I'm going to consummate this marriage so fucking hard you're going to walk with a limp on that beach in Fiji."

I burst out laughing, wrapping my arms around him as his mouth slowed and eventually simply kissed a path from my shoulder to my cheek. "Promise?" I asked.

He sighed, kissing my lips once. "Promise. Now, how many hours do I have to play nice with our crazy family before we can leave and I can put my hands all over your naked skin?"

I looked over his shoulder, searching for a kitchen

clock, but all I saw was at least twenty faces, all staring wide-eyed and slack-jawed at us. One waiter was so stunned by Bennett's display that a stack of plates slowly slid from his grasp and shattered on the floor.

Following the deafening crash of porcelain on tile, the kitchen finally returned to motion: people running for brooms and dustpans, the head chef barking out orders again. Bennett and I apologized quietly and ducked out of the kitchen and to the edge of the veranda, watching our guests begin to collect near the disaster of the lawn, taking appetizers from passing waitstaff.

I stretched to reach Bennett's ear and said, "We just got married. That means you're legally my manservant now."

His long fingers dug into my sides, tickling me as he reached with his other hand to grab a flute of champagne from a tray and handed it to me. He took one for himself and quietly clinked my glass. "To us, my wife."

"To us."

We watched the wedding party begin to assemble for the photos and Max waved at us to come join them. Sara turned around, laughing at something George said, and I caught a full view of her dress.

Bennett must have seen it at the same time as I did, because I heard him suck in a huge breath. He took my hand and began guiding me to the area where the photographer had set up the tripod.

"About that," I began.

"Yeah," he said glumly. "About that."

"What the fuck happened, Mills?"

He slid his eyes to me at the use of my last name and said, "Apparently the van door was open when we left the cleaners." He smiled at the straggler guests heading to the patio for cocktails, and maneuvered me on the outskirts of the crowd to avoid getting stopped every three feet on our way to the photographer. "And before you ask, Will tripped and dropped my wedding ring in the parking lot when he was trying to show me how good a job they did polishing it. I'm about two seconds from pulling you into the bathroom and forcing you onto your knees, so if you blow up at me or flip out about the dress or ring or the flooded lawn now, you will only convince me you need a dick in your mouth, and you'll completely derail the agenda for our wedding day: pictures, dancing, food, dancing, cake, long hard fucking. Watch what you say next, Ryan."

When we returned to the party, music pulsed from large speakers on the veranda and I felt high, drunk, outright *giddy* from the day and the man at my side. He never let go of my hand, but even if he'd tried I wouldn't let him. I loved the sharp press of his (dented) wedding ring between my fingers, and the way he kept lifting my hand to kiss it but really it seemed like he just wanted to make sure his ring was still there.

We made the rounds and spent the next couple of hours greeting everyone who came and getting lost in introductions and hellos. The guests ate the appetizers, and everyone seemed to get a little day-drunk and wild. Truth be told, it was overwhelming having so many people here. By the time dinner was served, the crowd was roaring, knives clinked against glasses almost every ten seconds in shameless bids to have Bennett kiss me.

Each time it grew a little dirtier until I worried he was going to clear the wedding table with a sweep of his arm and lay me down on it. But when Kristin told us the band would be starting our first dance song soon, and a symphony of knives tinkling against crystal rang out, Bennett simply leaned over and said, "If you put your tongue in my mouth again, I'm leaving this fucking wedding and taking you to bed, Mrs. Ryan."

"Well, I'll then keep it chaste, Mr. Mills. Because I want cake."

His eyes fell closed and he leaned forward, gently touching his lips to mine. How did he manage to blend sweet and commanding so seamlessly?

We walked to the center of the dance floor amid hushed silence. The first few chords of the song began and Bennett gave me a devilish grin before pulling me close with both hands gripping my ass. The room exploded in raucous cheers and I looked up at him, shaking my head as if it bothered me.

It so fucking didn't.

Without shoes, I was so much shorter than he was, and still sometimes hated not being able to see him eye to eye, even when we were dancing at our wedding. I stood on my tiptoes, swayed in his arms, and after only about half a minute I felt him reach around my waist and lift me so we were face-to-face, my feet dangling several inches off the ground.

"Better?" he asked, his voice gruff.

"Much." I twisted my fingers in his hair and leaned to slide my mouth over his.

Camera flashes exploded around us and I could imagine hundreds of pictures of Bennett holding me, spinning me slowly, my still-dirty feet telling anyone who would look at the picture in the future what kind of wedding day we'd had: perfect.

The song drew to an end, but it was several long beats after the final notes before Bennett put me down.

"I love you," he said, letting his eyes roam my entire face before coming to settle on my lips.

"I love you, too."

"Holy shit. You're my *wife*."

Laughing, I said, "We're married. That's *insane*. Who let this happen?"

He didn't even break a smile. Instead, his eyes grew heavy, his voice even lower. "I'm going to disrespect the *fuck* out of you later."

The entire surface of my skin felt flushed and silvery.

He released me, letting me slide down his body and

groaning quietly as my hip pressed against the length of his cock, half hard already. "I'm tempted to disrespect you now," he said. "But my wife wanted *cake*."

We drifted apart a little as another song started and I felt my father's hand press to my back. Bennett turned, taking his mother in his arms. As we danced with our parents, we caught each other's eyes over their shoulders and grinned, giddy. I felt like closing my eyes and letting out the loudest, happiest shout ever heard.

"Your mom would have had a great time today," Dad said, kissing my cheek.

I nodded, smiling. I missed my mother in this sort of hollow-throb way. She hadn't ever been the cool mom, or the fashionable mom; she was the sweet mom, the hugger mom, the overprotective mom. She would have hated Bennett at first, and the thought made me laugh out loud. Mom would have assumed he was a prick and that I could find someone more giving, more connected, more emotionally available. And then she would have seen him look at me in an unguarded moment, would have seen him trace a fingertip from my temple to my chin, or kiss the back of my hand when he didn't think anyone was looking, and realize I'd found the one man other than my dad who loved me more than anything on the planet.

Catching Bennett in these private moments had been what won my father over to Bennett's side, eventually. After our disastrous Christmas visit to Bismarck over a year ago, where Dad grilled Bennett endlessly and finally walked in on me riding him like a rowdy cowgirl in my childhood bed, Dad came to stay with us in New York for a week. Bennett, predictably, had been working like a fiend for the first few days, and Dad grumbled endlessly about how a man should provide for his family not only in material ways but also emotional.

But then one night, when Bennett got home well after midnight and Dad got up out of bed to get some water, he found us on the couch, my head in Bennett's lap and his fingers running gently through my hair as he listened to me ramble on about every detail of my day. Bennett had been exhausted, but, as usual, he insisted I spend time with him, no matter how late. Dad admitted the next morning that he had stood, mesmerized, watching us for a full five minutes before he remembered himself and left to get his water.

I caught him giving Bennett a look over my shoulder and then heard my husband's deep, real laugh—the one that bubbled up from low in his belly and came out sounding like the quietest, happiest sound.

"What are you two up to?" I asked my dad, pulling back to look at him.

"Just giving my new son some nonverbal advice."

I gave my father a warning look and then caught Bennett's attention as my father turned to me. His eyes twinkled with amusement. "Ask your husband what that was all about."

Dad pulled me into a hug, kissing my cheek, before Bennett came to my side, bending to whisper, "Your dad just indicated he wants five grandkids."

My screech of horror was drowned out by the heavy bass blasting through the speakers, signaling to the guests that the real party had started. Crowds rushed to the dance floor and we took the opportunity to go get a drink of water. Will passed us on our way, flanked by my aunts.

They sandwiched him between them good-naturedly and Will's head fell back in laughter. "For the love of God, Hanna, where *are* you?" he yelled.

Across the room she lowered her fruity drink, held up her hand decorated with a beautiful engagement ring, and called out, "Is that what this ring means? That I come to your rescue?"

He nodded fervently, shouting, "Yes!"

Finally, after a nice, long bit of staring at the poor boy, Hannah walked to him and pulled him away from my laughing aunts and into her arms. I smiled, turning back to Bennett.

"Can we leave now?" he asked, eyes dropping to my mouth.

The crowd had barely thinned, and I knew the party would probably continue on for another few hours, but right then all I wanted was to get upstairs and get my husband out of his tux.

"One more hour," I said, pulling back his jacket sleeve to glance at his watch. It was only eight thirty. "One more hour and then I'm all yours."

—⁂—

After what ended up being three hours—three hours of dancing and drunken toasts, of Max and Will carrying Bennett to the bar for a final round of "man shots," of pure, wild celebration—Bennett came up behind me at the bar where I stood talking to Henry and Mina, and slid his arms around my waist.

"Now," he whispered, kissing my ear.

I leaned back into him, smiling at my brother- and sister-in-law. "I think that's my cue."

There were no flower petals to throw in our wake, no handfuls of rice. Instead, Will and Henry grabbed handfuls of cocktail napkins and drunkenly chucked them at us as we ducked away from the bar and waved to our guests.

"Good night everyone! Thanks for coming!" I called out above the catcalls and whistles.

Bennett pulled me forward, waving over his shoulder. "Let's go."

"It was so good to see you all!" I yelled, still waving to our family and friends.

He practically dragged me away before lifting me and throwing me over his shoulder. The approval of our guests was communicated with roaring applause and another stack of napkins that caught Bennett in the back of the head.

He carried me all the way to the lobby and then slid me down his body, kissing my neck, my chin, my lips. "Ready?"

I nodded. "So ready."

But when I turned toward the elevators, he stopped me with a big hand wrapped around my forearm. And then his other hand pulled a blindfold out of his pocket.

"What . . . ?" I asked, a wary smile spreading slowly across my face. "What are you doing with that in the *lobby*?"

"I'm whisking you off somewhere."

"But we have a room upstairs," I whined quietly. "With a big giant bed and several of your ties to get kinky with, and," I dropped my voice, "the bottle of lube in the drawer."

He laughed, bending to run his nose along my jaw. "There's also a duffel bag in the limo outside that has several of my ties to get kinky with, the bottle of lube from the drawer, and a few other things."

"What other things?"

"Trust me," he said.

"Where are we going?" I asked, tripping after him when he tugged my hand and led me forward.

"Trust me."

"Do we have to fly?"

He playfully smacked my ass, growling, "Christ, woman, *trust me*," in my ear.

"Am I going to have orgasms tonight?"

He turned pulled me close to his side and said, "That's the plan. Now shut up."

Chapter Eight

Bennett helped me climb into the back of the limo and then slipped the blindfold over my face, tying it firmly behind my head. It was wide and *tight;* the bastard had anticipated my plan to peek, and the silken fabric covered half my face. I was left in total darkness.

But beside me, I could sense when he shifted closer, could smell the clean, crisp sagey smell of him when he leaned in, sucked gently on my collarbone.

"Are you going to fuck me in this car?" I asked, reaching out blindly for him. I found his arm and pulled it around me.

His rumbling chuckle vibrated along my collarbones, from one side to the other, and I felt him reach for the hem of my wedding dress and slowly drag it up my legs.

Bennett's fingertips tickled their way past my knee, along the inside of my thigh and to the thin white lace barely covering my pussy. He slid a knuckle under the fabric, dragging it back and forth over the already-slick skin beneath.

"Fuck," he hissed. "*Goddamnit*, Chlo." He pulled back, sliding two fingers into me, pumping them deep. "I'm not feeling particularly gentle tonight."

Arching my neck, I gave his mouth better access to the most vulnerable part of my throat, whispering, "Good. I don't want you slow and sweet."

"But it's our *wedding* night," he argued with mock sincerity. "Shouldn't I gently lay you on a feather bed and bring you endless, loving pleasure?"

I reached for his hand, pressed it harder into me. "You can do that when I'm bruised and sore afterwards, in the middle of the night."

His laugh was so dark, and communicated such barely restrained need that it sent shivers down my back. I felt his breath on my ear when he asked, "So I have permission to be rough?"

I nodded, my throat suddenly dry. "Encouragement, even."

"Maybe a little filthy?" When I answered with a nod, he growled, "*Tell* me."

I exhaled, a shaking, tense breath. "I want you filthy. I want you wild and impatient tonight. It's how I feel."

He twisted his wrist, and pushed a third finger into me so deep I felt the cool of his wedding ring against my skin, and I cried out from the sensation of the pressing metal, of being stretched tight. His thumb made teasing, maddening circles just around my clit, expertly never quite touching exactly where I wanted it. Traffic sounds grew to a crescendo and then ebbed into silence, and the steady thump of bridge spacers sounded beneath the wheels.

"Are we leaving Coronado?"

"Yes."

"Are we getting on a plane?" I asked again.

"Does my hand not feel good?" Irritation simmering in his voice.

". . . what?" I asked, confused.

"Are you distracted by the street, rather than the three fingers currently *fucking* you?"

"I—?"

He pulled his hand out and reached for my shoulders, pulling me off the seat and dragging me so I kneeled on the floor. I felt him shift around to pull me closer, and I realized I was positioned between his legs. The sound of his belt, his zipper, and his pants being shoved down his hips cut through the quiet.

"Come here," he said on an exhale, cupping the back of my head. *"Suck."*

Despite the single rough word, his touch grew careful as I began to lower my mouth over him, as if he wasn't sure how to blend his pent-up need to come with the reality of our brand-new marriage. We'd talked for cumulative hours about how things would be in this very moment—the two of us finally alone, married, and faced with the reality that it might be different—but now that we were in it, I could tell Bennett was a little torn.

We'd said *no way* would it feel different: it was just two rings, just a piece of paper.

We'd said we'd never stop being hard on each other, or start having easily bruised feelings.

We'd promised anything could always happen between us in the bedroom. We swore we'd never hold back, or be afraid to ask for whatever we needed.

But as I worked his length with my lips and my tongue, I could sense that Bennett's hands were fisted at his sides, not in my hair. His hips were pressed firmly into the seat beneath him, instead of rising up, arching toward my mouth.

So I did the first thing that came to mind: with a quiet sucking sound, I pulled my mouth off his cock and sat back on my heels.

His breaths came out in sharp gusts, but other than the sound of the road passing beneath us, the car fell silent.

Finally, his voice rose from the quiet in a controlled rumble: "What happened?"

What happened? So tame, Bennett.

In this moment, I hated not seeing his face, but I knew he understood the point I was making when he took a deep breath and asked, "Why the *fuck* did you stop?"

There he is.

"You know why."

Strong hands lifted me off my heels and sat me back until my butt hit the floor of the limo and my spine rested on the seat opposite him. One of Bennett's knees planted on the seat beside my head and without saying a word, he pressed the crown of his cock to my lips, forcing my mouth open.

"*Suck,*" he said, and this time the word was coated in anger and need. I barely had time to adjust to the feel of him before a tight fist curled in my hair, holding me steady as he began to move in short jabs, not going too deep, at least not yet. Finally, his hands released my hair and left me only long enough to frame the side of my face, holding me steady for his longer, deeper strokes.

The car rolled to a stop and Bennett slammed a palm on the intercom button, managing a sharp "Wait here" before returning his hand to my face, groaning hoarsely.

His rumbling "*Fuck,* Chlo" sparked my lust, and I reached up to wrap my arms around his hips, whimpering at the powerful snap of his thrusts, the hard contractions of muscles in his ass.

I couldn't see a thing, but each time he moved deeply and I felt the soft hair against my face, I wanted to suck as hard as I could so that when he pulled back I would wring as much pleasure out of this moment as I could for him. I felt desperate to give him this.

"So fucking good," he said, his voice raspy, and I could tell from his movements that he was growing close. "Those perfect fucking lips. Feeling your tongue on me."

I slid one hand between us, cupped his balls, and stroked just behind, teasing.

"Yes," he hissed, hips jerking.

With a final push inside, he came, cock rigid and releasing his orgasm down my throat. He cried out as I swallowed around him, slowing his movements until only the tip of him rested against my tongue. I tilted my head up to him when he pulled out, and felt the soft glance of his thumb across my bottom lip.

Wordlessly, Bennett reached down and adjusted my blindfold before bending and kissing me deeply, his tongue sliding over mine.

"Tell me you like my taste," he whispered.

"I *love* your taste."

And then he pulled my dress up, moving his hand between my legs and under the lace of my underwear, as if confirming what I'd said was true.

"I fucking *love* your mouth." He leaned forward, laughing against my lips. "And I love fucking your mouth."

His touch was gentler now, exploring rather than giving pleasure. He grunted quietly, moving his hand away from me, and I heard the rustle of fabric as he pulled up his pants, straightened his clothing.

Taking my hand, he murmured, "Come on, Mrs. Ryan. We're here."

———

We were definitely in a hotel. I could tell by the sounds of elevators, suitcases rolling across travertine floors. I could hear the way voices grow hushed as we walked past, and I imagined how we must look: Bennett carrying a blind-folded and barefoot bride in his arms and with a duffel bag full of who-knows-what slung over his shoulder, carrying me barefoot and blindfolded in my wedding dress.

"Are we in a hotel?"

"Shh," he whispered, lips to my temple. "We're almost there."

He carried me as if I weighed nothing, his strides even and steady. I pressed my lips to his neck and asked, "Is everyone looking at us?"

He turned his head, laughing quietly in my ear. "Definitely."

Once we stepped into the elevator, it smelled familiar. Was it possible we were back at the Hotel Del and he had just done an elaborate ruse to trick me? But if he did, why?

We rode up in silence and I adjusted my grip on his neck, trying to listen to the number of floors we passed, to any sign of where we were. Beneath my knees, his left hand squeezed me reassuringly.

"You okay?" he asked.

I nodded just as the elevator dinged and the doors opened, but Bennett didn't move. I realized there'd been someone else in there with us. How had it been for them, I wondered, to be watching us as we went up to wherever our final destination was, knowing we were clearly headed to our wedding night?

When we reached another floor, Bennett stepped out and carried me down what felt like the longest hallway ever.

"I want you inside me," I said into the warm skin of his neck.

"Soon."

"You won't make me wait?"

"I only want to get you there and naked. The plan beyond that is pretty self-explanatory."

Something about the walk felt familiar, some turn and body position, and suddenly it hit me.

Of course.

Of course.

He came to a stop, maneuvered so he could pull a key from his pocket, and opened the door.

I didn't even have to take off my blindfold to know.

Carefully, he put me down and I reached up, slipping the satin up and off my face. Yes. It was the room we'd stayed in at the W more than two years ago—the exact one. The same couch, the same bed, the same balcony, the same small kitchenette. Although, now it had a new, no-longer-broken desk.

The room where we first knew—really *knew*—that I was his and he was mine.

I could feel Bennett watching me, gauging my reaction, but I'd been so overwhelmed with emotion all week that I felt a little numb, almost as if on top of the family around us, the wedding, the vows, and how much I needed to feel him, my mind clamped shut and I started to feel dizzy.

He stepped behind me, kissing my neck. "You okay?"

"Yeah."

"We never did lose what we found in this room," he said, bending now and kissing my shoulder. "In fact, we turned it into the happiest hate-love of all time."

"We sure did." I turned to look at him, wondering if now was when he tore my dress off and fucked me face-down on the floor.

But his eyes were clear, careful. He stepped closer, bent to kiss my jaw. "You smell so fucking good."

"What's going on? I thought you were going to be rowdy."

"Fucking your mouth in the car helped take the edge off."

I closed my eyes, feeling memories storm into my thoughts.

"I've never done anything close to this and I don't know how to navigate it anymore," I'd said.

"I told you. I haven't been with anyone else since we started this," he'd said.

"That doesn't mean you won't take a room key if it's put in your hand."

"Let's call a truce for one night. I just need tonight," he'd pled, and given me three desperate kisses.

I opened my eyes. "How much of the first night in here are we going to re-create?"

He shrugged and when he smiled, he looked so young, almost innocent. "I think we'll skip the fight in the bathroom, but I definitely hope you wake me up with your mouth on my cock." He leaned forward, kissing me once and then pulling back to study my face. "Honestly, Chlo, I just want you out of this dress. I feel like we haven't been skin to skin in months."

I nodded without speaking, still overwhelmed and exhaling in relief when Bennett's broad hands slid across my bare back, unbuttoning and pushing my dress down my sides, holding it up just enough for me to step out of the skirts. I turned back around to face him, wearing only a tiny strapless bra and the smallest thong I think I'd ever worn in my life.

Without a word, he reached for me with lightning-quick hands and shredded the panties, and then reached up to my chest, gripped my bra in one hand, and savagely tore it from my body. Reflexively, I crossed my arms in front of me, my pulse hammering.

"You had other things you were going to put on for me tonight?" he asked, nodding to the bag he'd dropped in the entryway.

"I did . . ."

He was already shaking his head. "You won't need them. Maybe in the morning, but not right now."

Bennett kissed my shoulder, running rough, impatient

hands over my breasts, my hips, my thighs. "Undress me now."

It was suddenly surreal to be standing bare before him like this. He'd seen me naked thousands of times, and God knows he'd bossed me around like this even more often. But this moment felt so *loaded*. It wasn't the easy instinctual sex we had every night. This was Bennett, undressing me and demanding to be similarly stripped so we could have *Married Sex* in a *Fancy Bed* in an *Emotionally Relevant Room*.

The words *wedding night, wedding night, wedding night* pounded through my head. Maybe this is exactly what he felt in the limo: the pressure of doing it right, making it memorable.

I tried to ignore the way my hand shook when I pulled at his tie and slid it from his collar, but he noticed and he grabbed both of my wrists in one hand. The other slid down my front and between my legs, parting me, sliding a long finger over my clit and dipping into where I was wettest.

"Why are you *shaking*, Mrs. Ryan?"

With a flash of irritation, I bit his bottom lip when he leaned closer for a kiss. But then I closed my eyes, enjoying for a few moments the way he slid his finger back and forth over the rise of my clit before he stopped, patiently waiting for an answer.

"I'm a little nervous, *Mr. Mills*," I admitted.

His eyes went wide, nostrils flaring as he released my

hands from his grip. "You? *You're* nervous?" He looked like he was on the verge of yelling or laughing, I wasn't sure which. "You're nervous with *me*?"

Shrugging, I said, "It's just—"

"You're *nervous*?" His tone had changed this time; amusement curled through the two, short words. He was definitely on the verge of laughing.

I removed his cuff links, dropping them on the carpet at our feet. "Are you making fun of me?"

He shook his head slowly, but with a devilish smile said, "Yes."

Taking his shirt in my fists, I pulled it open, hearing the pop of the buttons as they tore free and skittered to the floor. "You're making fun of your bride on her *wedding* night?"

His expression straightened and his brow smoothed as I ran my greedy hand down his chest. "Of course I am."

"What kind of monster are you?" I teased, lightly scratching his stomach.

His answering smile tilted up one half of his perfect mouth. "The kind that's going to fuck you so hard it'll look like your legs were put on backwards."

I laughed, playfully shoving him, and he fought his own smile before bending to kiss me roughly, pressing his tongue into my mouth, sucking, and biting at my lips. "Come on, Chlo. I think we both know I'm pretty easy," he murmured. "Tend to my cock and the night is a success."

I ran my hands down his torso, feeling every dip and

hard ridge, and shivering when he bent and sucked my jaw, growling into my neck. I pressed into him, loving the feel of his hungry hands down my back, grabbing my ass.

"Get over your ridiculous nerves and fucking *undress* me," he hissed, kicking off his shoes and bending to peel off his socks.

I gave his zipper an impatient tug and pushed his dress pants and boxers down to the floor. With his hands on my waist, Bennett backed me to the bed. And then he kneeled in front of me, bracing his hands on my hips and leaning forward to kiss my navel. His wedding ring winked in the dim light of the bathroom.

"We're married," he said quietly, pressing another kiss to my belly button. "I'm your safe place. I've always been your safe place."

I slid my hands into his hair, pulling gently and knowing he was right. I'd been my best and worst self with this man, and he only loved me more the more real I was with him. No place was safer for me than with Bennett.

He moved his mouth from one hip to the other, up my ribs, tongue sweeping over my breasts, teeth pulling gently at their peaks. And then he rose to his feet as he kissed up my neck until he towered in front of me, hair hanging over his brow, eyes dark and predatory.

"How many times have we been together like this?"

I shrugged. "Maybe a million?"

"Are you still nervous?" he asked quietly, lifting my left hand and kissing my wedding ring.

I watched his tongue dart out, licking my finger, and whispered, "Not anymore."

His expression grew serious. "Are you happy we did this?"

Nodding, I managed a hoarse "I'm *giddy.*" He bent, kissing me, and I said into his smiling mouth, "I think you're the best thing that's ever happened to me."

" 'You think?' " Reaching up, he pressed both hands to my face, sliding a thumb inside my mouth. His lips twisted into a dark, teasing smile. " 'You *think?*' "

I nodded, pressing my teeth into his knuckle.

"*Suck* it," he growled, and then shivered when I wrapped my lips around him, circling him with my tongue.

Between us, he was so hard his whole body was tense, hands shaking at the sides of my face. "Look at me."

I shivered, unable to break my attention from where his cock arched straight up between us.

"Look at me," he ground out.

I blinked up to him and he slid his thumb deeper into my mouth, pressing down against my tongue. He groaned quietly, watching as he slowly withdrew his digit; I bit down so his skin dragged against my teeth.

A calm silence settled between us. Bennett's expression straightened and he simply stared down at me, studying every part of my face as he swept the wet pad of his thumb back and forth across my bottom lip.

"Married," he said quietly, as if only to himself.

I loved his honest, expressive hazel eyes, his smart mouth, and his carved, stubborn jaw. I loved his tousled hair and the heavy dip of his Adam's apple when he swallowed. I loved his broad chest, sculpted arms, and the world's best naughty fingers. I loved his abdomen, his hips, and every long, thick inch of him pressing urgently between us.

But more than any of that, I loved his intelligence, his composure, his loyalty, his sense of humor. And I loved how he loved me.

Tilting his head, he asked, "What are you thinking, Mrs. Ryan?"

"I'm thinking how it's a good thing I love your body so much that I can put up with your disappointing brain."

He spread his hands around my waist and lifted me, tossing me onto the mattress.

"If you think I'm going to put up with that smart mouth of yours now that we're married . . ." he began, crawling up the bed and hovering over me.

"Then I'm right?" I finished for him, reaching to wrap my hand around the back of his neck.

He bent to kiss me, giving me a lopsided smile. "Yeah, actually."

I'd often had this feeling when I was alone with Bennett that time somehow *melted* and the entire world outside simply dissolved into nothing. I'd been nervous with the anticipation of tonight, but once his weight settled over me—and his mouth moved to my neck, my shoulders, my breasts—instinct took over. I slid my palms up his back and over his shoulders and gasped as he returned to me, his tongue touching mine, pushing and demanding. The sounds of his excitement vibrated inside my mouth and down my neck as he grew wilder, needing to kiss and taste everything, all at once.

I suspected I knew this man better than I knew my own mind. I knew how to touch him, how to love him, how to get him to do anything and everything to my body. And so when his hands spread my thighs apart, thumbs circling and meeting in the middle to glide over my clit, and his eyes focused on my face as his lips clamped over the peak of my breast—studying, commanding, hungry for my pleasure—I lost any sense of anxiety over the night and knew we would forever be the fevered combination of Bennett and Chloe. Mr. Ryan and Miss Mills. Mr. Mills and Mrs. Ryan. Husband and wife. Bastard and bitch.

Kneeling between my legs, his hands framed my hips and he watched as he slid over my wet skin, before resting the head of his cock on my navel. I could feel my pulse thundering in my throat, and I lifted my hips, suddenly impatient for this, wanting to feel his weight on top of me, hear his desperate sounds in my ear.

"Should I say something profound before we begin?" he asked, smiling down at me.

"You can try," I said, scratching down his stomach. "But I wouldn't want you to hurt yourself."

With a light pinch to my nipple, he bent low, nipping at my jaw. "I love you anyway."

As he slid into me, I shook, crying out sharply at the relief before gasping, "I love you anyway, too."

"It feels so *fucking* good."

"I know."

I pressed my palms to his ass, feeling the contracting muscles, pulling him deeper into me and rising to meet his every push. Bennett's lips moved across my cheeks, aimless, to my ears and my mouth. Down my chin to my neck. His words came out broken and desperate.

So much

Oh, God, Chlo, I don't

Let me hear

Let me hear you

Tell me what you're feeling, tell me

Tell me what you want

I sucked at his neck, watching his shoulders bunch as he moved and moved and moved over me. "I want faster. Closer. More. *Please.*"

He pushed up onto his knees between my legs, gripping my thigh and pushing my legs farther apart. "Fucking hell, Chloe, you're so beautiful."

I groaned, feeling the heavy drag of him sliding inside me; the pleasure was amplified by the way his eyes seemed to caress my skin.

"Reach down," he whispered. "Feel where I move in you."

I did what he asked, letting his cock move over my fingertip as he slid in and out.

He bent low. "Tell me what you feel."

"Wet," I answered, looking up at him. "Hard."

His gaze burned and he stared down at my fingers on him. When he smiled, he looked dangerous, and it made my heart slam into my chest.

"I know," he said. He took in my tangled hair, picked up one of my dirty feet, and slid my ankle up his hip. "You're a mess, you greedy fucking girl."

He slowed, pulling almost all the way out until I panicked and wrapped my legs around his waist. It felt like a match had been lit inside my belly and it burned, spreading like wildfire down between my legs, serving only to increase the impatient need I felt.

As if sensing how close I was, Bennett pushed back into me, focused now on getting me there. He was sweaty, his hair damp from exertion, and a drop fell from his forehead onto my chest, and then another.

"Tell me how good it is," he said, his voice low and commanding.

"I . . . I . . ."

With a sharp jab of his hips, he thrust harder into me. "Tell me, Chloe, how good the *fucking* is."

I couldn't answer, already starting to dissolve. He was wild: rough touches and punishing thrusts, flipping me on the bed and taking, taking, taking. My eyes closed, my cheek resting against the cool blankets when his hands fisted in my hair, forcing my head back as his mouth found my neck, each labored exhale sending waves of warm breath across my dampened skin. He kissed along my shoulders, his tongue reaching out to taste me, his teeth nipping and dragging along my skin. I arched my back, angling my hips to meet each push of his hips. My arms reached out, hands twisting in the sheets, my entire body shaking with the need to let go.

But he didn't give me what I needed. Instead, he teased and took, and took some more, and then finally, with a determined set to his jaw, and more desperate need in his eyes than I'd seen in days, leaned in close, circling over me and giving—giving, *giving*—me an orgasm so intense it left me shaking and near tears in his arms. What had built in my belly to a low, heavy ache exploded up my spine and spilled like liquid heat into my limbs until my toes were curling. *Fuck*, it had been so long since I'd felt that: my body coming around *him*, trying to draw him in, greedy for every commanding inch. I worried my heart might smash through my ribs with how hard it was beating.

The relief in the epiphany—he *wouldn't* change, he could only ever be this greedy, demanding Bastard—was such intense relief that I finally did give in to my emotions, shaking in his arms, clutching him until I caught my breath. But when I asked him what he wanted, and he groaned, "I want you to take over. I want you to wreck me," I smiled, slowly climbing on top of him.

He was sweaty, hair dripping onto the pillow beneath him, and muscles bunched and coiled beneath smooth, tan skin. His eyes saw nothing in the room but me, flaring hotly at the anticipation of what I'd do. I looked him over: freshly fucked hair, blazing hazel eyes, lips so wrecked from my mouth and skin they were red and chafed. His pulse hammered in his neck, and I dragged one finger down the sweaty center of his chest, over the vulnerability of his solar plexus, down to his belly button, and then followed the trail of hair leading to his cock, still wet from me, still hard and perfect and practically pulsing for my touch.

"No," I said, running my hands back up his torso, reveling in the feel of him. It really wasn't fair. In a perfect world, Bennett Ryan would be a manwhore so that more women would get to appreciate this body.

But let's be honest: *Fuck that.*

"'No'?" He repeated, eyes narrowing.

"You wore me out," I said, shrugging. "I'm tired."

"Chloe. Put the fucking *dick* in your *mouth.*"

"You'd like that?"

His nostrils flared, hips arching up into me seeming without intention on his part. "Now, Chloe."

"Say please."

Sitting up beneath me abruptly, he growled, "Chloe, *please* choke on my dick."

I burst out laughing, curling into him and sliding my hands into that mess of sweaty, amazing hair. Leaning forward, I covered his mouth with mine, sucking and wet, hungry for the taste of him, the feel of his sounds. I kissed him for making me laugh, for making me scream. I kissed him for being the only person who truly understood me, for being so impossibly like me in some ways it was a wonder we ever agreed on anything. I kissed him for being Bennett Ryan, *my* Beautiful Bastard.

Against my lips, I felt him smiling, heard the quiet vibration of his laugh, muffled by my mouth. "I love you," he said.

Pulling back, I nodded, whispering, "Me, too. I love you a scary amount."

"Then seriously, Mrs. Ryan," he said. "Put my dick in your mouth."

Acknowledgments

It's surreal to be done writing the *Beautiful* series less than a year after we sold it to Gallery. We're excited to move on to something new, but it's bittersweet because we've really had the time of our lives writing these saucy books. We're going to miss these crazy characters.

We want to begin by thanking everyone who has made the journey with us in these books—from *Beautiful Bastard* to *Beautiful Beginning*—we have had the most fun doing this with you. Thank you, truly, for buying and reading our books. We're still writing with just as much silliness and passion as when we started this adventure. We sincerely hope you love what comes next.

Our agent, Holly Root, had a sixth sense about Gallery's Adam Wilson; we think she just knew that he would be a perfect fit for these books, and for us. We've said it in every book, and we'll say it again: thanks to both of you for being exactly who you are, because you're exactly what we needed. Holly, you're hands-on whenever we need you, and hands-off when you trust us to do our thing. Adam, you've made these books so much better and distracted us from your plethora of margin notes by making them hilarious (and spot-on). Look for the petal cupcakes heading your way. We like you. We like you a lot.

What Jen Bergstrom said to us in Orlando is true: Simon & Schuster's Gallery imprint works like a big family, and we've felt that from day one. Thanks to Adam for bringing us to the table. And to Carolyn Reidy, Louise Burke, Jen Bergstrom: thank you for taking us on with such investment and enthusiasm. Thank you, Kristin Dwyer and Mary McCue in publicity, for your tireless work on these six novels in only ten months (and also for just being badass and irresistibly adorable and our preciouses). Thank you, Liz Psaltis and Ellen Chan, for the amazing work on the marketing side. Thank you, Carly Sommerstein, our production editor, who we've sent into the trenches with our quick turnarounds. We've loved every single cover—thank you, Lisa Litwack and John Vairo!—the Gallery art department really hit it out of the park designing them. Thank you to our first copy editor for the joke that will never stop being funny. And a preemptive thanks to whoever volunteers to always ensure Adam eats the cupcake with the candy bone on it. Yes, we're twelve.

Lauren Suero, you've been so good to us and to Team Beautiful from day one. Thank you for running our social media, following every bit of *Beautiful* news, and keeping us buoyed in our text box. Jennifer Grant, thank you for help on the promo side and with the website. What you've done for us is seriously amazing. Thank you to every blogger who has reviewed us, recced us, tweeted us, and talked about us. Your support means so much!!

To our *Beautiful* pre-readers—Erin, Martha, Tonya, Myra, Tawna, Anne, Kellie, Katy, and Gretchen—thank you for giving us your eyes, your time, your thoughts. These books have been ridiculously fun for us to write, and we hope they've been even a fraction as fun to read. We really do love it when you fill our box with happy reactions and constructive criticism. Hopefully your eyes aren't tired, because we have lots more books to come.

Of course, we want to thank the fandom, because it's where we met and where we remain. In the past nearly five years, you've become more than a community we joined to read and write fanfic. Collectively, you have become some of our closest friends and a group of women about whom we care very deeply. Thanks for being excited for us and for sharing your own victories with us along the way. We hope you feel pride in our happiest moments the way we feel it in each of yours. We adore you all.

Our families and friends have listened to us speak about almost nothing else for the past year, and not once have you been anything other than excited and supportive. We're grateful, and we're lucky. Thanks for being proud of us, and seeming to enjoy the ride as much as we have. You're either completely adorable in your excitement, or very good actors.

Husbands: we love you. We'll do a better job telling you in person. Hell, maybe we'll even show you. (On that note, thanks for giving us such cute and wonderful kiddos.)

To Christina, {insert sentimental quote here, really just an excuse to smell your hair}

To Lo, {insert sappy, adoring thoughts here, including how I could watch you make tabbed and color-coded spreadsheets all day}

Beautiful
BASTARD

A Novel

CHRISTINA LAUREN

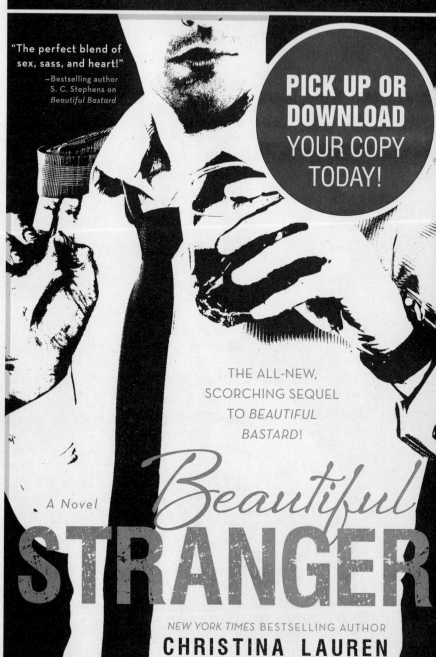

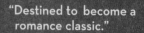